Veronica feels so unwanted—
except by the Gold Girls. . .

Lexi looked at Abbie, then at me. "Every girl here had to pass an initiation to get into the Gold Girls," she said.

"We all stole something at the mall that was worth over a hundred dollars," Julie explained.

"Oh, cool!" Abbie said eagerly.

I was shocked. I had never stolen anything in my life. Were they going to ask me to steal, too? I would say no, I decided. Absolutely. But then I'd never be a Gold Girl. Well, so what? I looked around at the circle of friends in their gold baseball jackets. They all belonged to each other. They were a part of something. With all my heart, I wanted to be a part of something, too.

But would I steal for it?

The
Initiation

*For the thousands of readers all over the
world who honor me with your letters and
photos, and your willingness to share your
hopes and dreams. You're the coolest!*

HOPE HOSPITAL

The Initiation

BY CHERIE BENNETT

Troll

CHAPTER 1

"Basically, I want a divorce," I told my two best friends, Cindy Winters and Tina Wu. We had just gotten into the Hope Hospital van that would take us on a field trip to a petting zoo on a farm just outside of town. My friends and I are all thirteen, and along with two of our friends, Brad Kennedy (who is also my cousin and Tina's boyfriend) and Trevor Wayne (who Cindy is totally in love with), we were chaperoning a group of ten little kids who were patients at the hospital.

"From who?" Cindy asked as she helped Jenny Pilton, a cute five-year-old girl recovering from a car accident, into her seat.

"Try to keep up, Cindy," I said seriously. "I want a divorce from my mother."

"But, Veronica," Tina said as she bounced into a seat next to Brad, "you can't divorce a parent. Can you?"

"I saw an old movie about it on TV the other night," I told her as I helped Heidi, Cindy's little sister, with her seat belt. "This girl's parents were fighting so much, and she was so sick of it, that she went to court to divorce them."

"But your parents are already divorced," Brad pointed out logically.

"The papers aren't final," I said quickly. "Besides, as you know, my mother is always so busy at the hospital that I talk to her even less than I talk to my father."

"But your dad is back in New York," Trevor said, shaking the hair out of his eyes.

"*He* calls me on the phone," I said. "*She* leaves me notes."

He's called you exactly four times since you moved to Hope, I told myself. But I wasn't about to admit that to anyone else.

As the van started up, I stared out the window and thought about how my mother and I had ended up moving to the tiny town of Hope, Michigan, and how very much my life had changed.

I was born in New York City, which I thought was the center of the entire universe. Both my parents are doctors. I went to private school and studied ballet from the time I was four years old. Adults were always telling my parents what a pretty girl I was—in that embarrassing way adults have of talking about you right in front of you as if you had suddenly gone deaf, dumb, and blind—but I didn't particularly think they were right. I'm thin and kind of tall, and I have long, straight brown hair. I do like my hair; that's one good thing.

Another thing people have told me ever since I can remember is that I'm too serious. I wish I could be as funny as Cindy, or as enthusiastic as Tina, but it just isn't me.

I was devastated—I mean truly devastated—when my parents told me they were getting a divorce. They never fought or anything. Now when I think back on it, I realize that they never laughed, either, or hugged or kissed, but I just thought that was normal.

And if that wasn't bad enough, my mother then informed me that she and I were moving to Hope, Michigan, which is so small you can barely find it on a map, so that she could be the new head of pediatrics—which is basically medical care for kids—at Hope Hospital.

I had to leave New York. My school. My ballet teacher. Everything.

And I didn't have any say in the matter.

Sometimes I think about that—how kids have no power. Adults get to call the shots. They get to tell you what to do twenty-four hours a day. It doesn't seem very fair to me. I pointed this out to my mother once, and she said that adults had life experience, which they used to guide children.

Well, pardon me, but I know quite a number of kids who are smarter than quite a number of adults, life experience or not.

So, we moved to Hope. The only good thing about it was that my cousin, Brad, who is fourteen, and my aunt and uncle lived there already. Brad is really great—cute, smart, and a great artist. He was born with a hole in his heart, and he gets sick a lot. He needs major surgery to fix it. And he doesn't want to have it. But that's another story.

Anyway, there I was in this little, tiny town where I absolutely did not want to be, going to Hope Middle School, where everyone had known everyone else forever (I might just as well have worn a neon sign that screamed NEW GIRL!). And I was miserable. Until I met Cindy Winters. Cindy is short for Cinderella—her parents had a disturbed sense of humor. She was in my class at school—this tiny, cute blonde, very funny and sarcastic, who was nice to me right away. I was too scared and miserable at first to be nice to her back, and I think she thought that I was a snob, which I assure you I am not.

Cindy's mom died of cancer years ago, and her dad is a pediatric social worker at Hope Hospital. Hope Hospital is kind of famous, especially for pediatric medicine.

Well, one day Cindy's little sister, Heidi, was in a terrible accident. She actually fell off the top of a Ferris wheel at a traveling amusement park. For a while no one even knew if Heidi would live. Even after she was out of the woods, she had to spend a really long time in the hospital. I started going there with Cindy, and that's where we both met Tina Wu.

Tina Wu is one of a kind. Cindy and I

both call her Tina Wu now, as if it's one name—we got this from Tina's grandmother, who lives with Tina and runs the entire Wu family. Tina is a little plump, with a darling round face, glossy black hair, and enough enthusiasm for ten people. She's an Asian-American from a big Chinese family. She's got lupus—this autoimmune disease—and she gets admitted to Hope Hospital now and then—but you wouldn't know anything was wrong with her unless she told you.

Tina is home-schooled by her mother, which may account for the fact that she is a hopeless romantic and kind of boy-crazy. I mean, she never gets to be with any boys at school. She and Brad really, really like each other. Only Tina isn't allowed to have a boyfriend yet, so she pretty much has to hide this fact from her family.

The truth of the matter is, I didn't have any really close friends in New York. Not like Tina and Cindy. Sometimes people think I'm a snob, but I'm not. Actually, sometimes I'm shy. And quiet. And very serious, which, let's face it, doesn't necessarily make a girl Miss Popularity, even if she is reasonably nice-looking.

But as different as we are, we had become

friends. Best friends. I had never really had one best friend before, let alone two. It was...well, it was wonderful.

Especially since I didn't really have a family anymore.

"How's my favorite foxy lady?" Jerome Winslow asked, leaning forward from his seat behind me.

Jerome is one of my favorite kids at the hospital. He's ten years old, African-American, very handsome and very smart, and he has bone cancer. In fact, when we met him, he had already lost one of his legs to the disease because the doctors had to amputate it to the knee to stop the cancer from spreading. There was a chance he would lose his other leg, too. His parents are both lawyers and Jerome goes to a ritzy private school, but he likes to pretend he is street-tough. He tells everyone he's in a gang, and he has his initial *J* shaved into his hair on the side of his head.

"Hey!" Tina cried from the seat across from him. "I thought I was your favorite!" She pretended to pout.

"Woman, you got your own man!" Jerome exclaimed, cocking his head at Brad. "What you want with two?"

"The same thing you want with two

girlfriends," Cindy told him with a laugh. "Or three. Or twenty."

"Hey, I can handle it," Jerome said seriously. "I got appetites." He turned to look at me. "You want to go out sometime?"

I smiled. "You ask me that every day, Jerome."

"We could go to an X-rated movie," he suggested. "I got fake ID."

"You're ten years old," I reminded him.

"So? Live fast, die young, and leave a good-looking corpse, I always say," he told me. He pulled some sunglasses out of his pocket and put them on at a jaunty angle.

I couldn't really smile at that. Not long ago a little girl with leukemia, Brianna, had died at Hope Hospital. She loved Jerome and had followed him everywhere. Also, there really was a chance that Jerome could die from his bone cancer.

But I tried hard not to think about that.

"Are we there yet?" Heidi called from her window seat.

"We're two blocks away from the hospital and you know it," Cindy said, reaching forward from her seat to tickle her little sister.

"I want to see lions and tigers!" Deena called out from the front of the van. Deena is six, and she has very serious diabetes that the doctors have a difficult time stabilizing.

"It's a petting zoo," I explained. "There are only animals there that you can pet."

"That's stupid," she said, flopping back into her seat. "It's a stupid zoo."

"Yeah, we want big animals!" Heidi agreed in a loud voice.

"Yeahhhh!" a little boy near the back added. "We want big monster animals!"

Sometimes this kind of thing happened. When one kid got a certain idea, everyone joined in.

"Hey, how about if we sing a song?" Tina asked quickly.

"Don't start on some stupid 'Farmer in the Dell,' now," Jerome warned, folding his arms.

"No, it's a great song," Tina insisted. "This is how it goes." She began to sing a song about hula dancers and popsicles— the lyrics were really silly, but the kids loved it and soon they were all singing.

"So, what is the deal with this divorce-your-mom thing?" Cindy asked, leaning over so I could hear her over the kids' singing.

I shrugged and brushed a strand of hair

out of my face. "She deserves it."

"Because she doesn't pay any attention to you?" Cindy asked.

"She's never home," I said. "She's always at the hospital. I see Miss Jenkins more than I see her."

Miss Jenkins is our housekeeper and my mother's assistant. She's worked for us forever. She came with us from New York. You'd think that after so many years I'd have some kind of personal relationship with her, but I don't. This is just the way it is.

"So, try hanging out at my crazy house for a while," Cindy suggested. "You'll want to run back to your mansion in The Hills so fast, you won't know what hit you."

Cindy's house is very small and, well, kind of shabby. Her dad doesn't make all that much money, and frankly he isn't very good at handling what money he has. Cindy and Heidi share a bedroom, and her older brother, Clark, has his own bedroom, but it's so small nothing can fit in there but a bed and a small dresser.

"I'm not complaining about being rich," I said.

"Oh, good," Cindy said, laughing. "Because I would gladly kill my brother to have just one of your family's millions."

Oh, I guess I forgot to mention that I am rich. Very rich. At least my mother is. She comes from a very, very wealthy family. We live in a huge house in a very upscale part of Hope called The Hills.

I hate it.

The house is always empty. It's silent. My mother is always at the hospital. Every night after Miss Jenkins serves dinner, she goes to the small private apartment she lives in, on the rear of our property. I could call her to come back over, but I never do. She leaves and I say goodbye and pretend that I am perfectly fine.

Then it is so quiet that I can hear my own heart. Beat. Beat. Beat.

Usually I turn on all four televisions as loud as I can, and then I do my homework and pretend the voices are my brothers and sisters, and they're just in another room.

Please don't tell anyone. I couldn't even admit this to Cindy and Tina Wu. I just couldn't. I mean, it's so pathetic.

And kind of a cliché, don't you think? The lonely little rich girl? The fact of the matter is, if you are rich, no one really wants to hear about your problems.

And I don't blame them.

"Last one out is a rotten egg!" Marielle called, her eyes shining. She is an eight-year-old African-American girl, very skinny, with sickle-cell anemia. She was sitting right behind the driver, next to Virginia Overton, the head nurse who was supervising the trip.

Virginia Overton is in her mid-forties, I would guess. She has a very deep voice and she's built like a truck. Tina calls her Virgin-for-Life Virginia.

I stopped daydreaming. We had just arrived at the petting zoo and everyone was clambering out of the van.

I helped the kids out, and then I helped Virginia unfold wheelchairs for the three kids who couldn't walk. Meanwhile Cindy went to buy our tickets.

"I want to see every single animal!" Deena cried with excitement.

"I knew her tune would change," Tina whispered to me with a wink.

"Can I hold your hand, Brad?" Amy Newton asked, looking up at Brad. Amy is nine, and she has Hodgkin's disease.

"The question is, can I hold *your* hand, Miss Amy?" he asked her solemnly, reaching out for her.

"Tell me he isn't the greatest guy on the

face of the earth," Tina said to me with a sigh.

"I got the tickets," Cindy said, hurrying back over to us. By the time she got there, we were all organized—everyone who needed them had crutches or a wheelchair, and everyone was eager to go.

"Okay, group, let's hit it!" Trevor said.

"Let's rock 'n' roll!" Jerome added, trying to look as fierce as possible. He still had his dark sunglasses on, and his baggy shorts fell over the stump that was his left leg.

Happily we all started toward the entrance gate.

"Oh, Mommy, look at that little boy!" a girl cried, pointing at Jerome. "He only has one leg!"

Jerome pretended not to hear, but I knew he did. So did everyone else. He just kept bopping along on his crutches.

"What's wrong with all those kids?" the little girl's brother asked.

"Shhhh!" their mother admonished him. "They're sick. Don't get too close to them." She moved her children to the other side of her and hurried away from us.

"Old bat," Jerome mumbled. "I ought to get my gang to ice her."

No one else said anything. I felt terrible for them. More than anything in the world, I wanted to say or do just the right thing to make the kids feel better, but my mind was completely blank.

"Hey!" Tina finally said. "We're the coolest, we're the baddest, right?"

"Right!" Cindy agreed. "We're so cool we don't care what anyone thinks! So let's go!"

Kids grabbed onto Tina and Cindy, holding their hands, their T-shirts, whatever they could get. I wished for the zillionth time that I could be more like them. They knew just how to inspire the kids, just what to say.

And I didn't.

No kids grabbed onto my hands. I pushed Marielle's wheelchair and tried not to care.

But I couldn't help wishing that once, just once, I would be the most popular one. The one who said or did exactly the right thing.

The one everybody loved.

CHAPTER 2

"Veronica, there's a phone call for you," Miss Jenkins said through the intercom speaker on my desk. Evidently she hadn't gone to her apartment yet.

It was four hours later. The kids ended up having a great time at the petting zoo. Cindy and Tina made it all so entertaining for them. After making sure all the kids were back in their rooms at the hospital, I called Miss Jenkins, who came to drive me home.

My mother, of course, was not home. I ate with Miss Jenkins, and then, even though it was Saturday, I went up to my room to do my homework.

Of course I turned all the TVs on first.

I used the remote control to turn down the sound and picked up the pink princess phone by my bed. "Hello?"

"Veronica? This is Lexi Stanton."

Lexi Stanton! Lexi Stanton was only the most popular girl in the entire eighth grade at Hope Middle School. She always looked perfect and she was the arbiter of everything cool. When Lexi wore baby barrettes in her hair, everyone decided they had to wear baby barrettes in their hair. When Lexi wore over-the-knee socks, every girl in school had to get over-the-knee socks. She had long sun-streaked blond hair, and she modeled part time in Detroit. I hadn't really talked to her much in school, but recently I had joined the advanced ballet class at Miss Faye's School of Dance, and Lexi was in my class. We talked a little sometimes, as we warmed up. Frankly, I was a much better dancer than she was.

And I had absolutely no idea why she was calling me.

"Hi," I said, sitting down on my bed.

"I guess you're surprised to hear from me," Lexi said in her confident voice.

"A little," I admitted.

"Well, I've been watching you," Lexi said. "That outfit you wore to school yesterday was really cute."

I tried to remember what I had worn to school the day before. Oh, yes. A short flippy white skirt with white tights and a white sweater with little pearl buttons on it. I had bought it at Saks Fifth Avenue in New York right before we moved.

"Thanks," I said. Was she calling me up to talk about my clothes?

"So, listen," Lexi continued, "next Saturday night I'm having this party. And I wanted to invite you."

I couldn't believe it. Lexi Stanton was inviting me to her party! I was flattered in spite of myself. I mean, everyone at Hope Middle School wanted to get invited to one of Lexi Stanton's parties. They were famous. Only the very coolest kids got invited. I had heard that her parents even left the house for a couple of hours and the kids got to do whatever they wanted.

"That's very nice of you," I said. My voice sounded forced and stilted to my own ears. I get that way sometimes when I'm nervous.

"Well, like I said, I've been watching you," Lexi said coolly. "You're cute and you've got great clothes. And you're a really great dancer."

"Thanks," I said happily.

"You might even be Gold material," Lexi added.

Gold material! Had she really said that? The Gold Girls was Lexi's secret, exclusive club, only everyone knew about it. On certain days they all wore gold clothes to school, and they all wore matching slender gold rings on their little fingers. Only six girls were Gold Girls. Only six girls in the entire school.

And she thought I might be Gold material?

"So you'll come?" Lexi asked.

"Sure," I said, trying not to sound too eager.

"I would have called you sooner," Lexi continued, "but you hang out with Cindy Winters, don't you?"

I wrapped the phone cord around my finger. "Yes..."

"Well, she's okay," Lexi said carelessly. "I mean, she's not a dweeb or anything. But...she's not all that cool, you know?"

"I really like Cindy," I said firmly.

"Oh, well, I don't know her all that well," Lexi said as if she could care less. "She's kind of young-looking, isn't she?"

"Cindy can't help it if she's small for her age," I pointed out.

"Yeah, whatever," Lexi said with a bored sigh. "So, I'll give you my address Monday at school and everything, okay?"

"Okay," I agreed, but something was starting to feel not quite right in my stomach. "I don't suppose...are you inviting Cindy?"

"Why would I do that?" she asked.

"You'd probably really like her if you knew her better," I explained.

"I'd have to *want* to know her better, wouldn't I?" Lexi asked snottily.

"I just...she might feel bad if I come to your party and she isn't invited," I explained, clutching the phone hard.

"You aren't serious," Lexi scoffed.

"I'm totally serious."

"So, what are you saying, you have to *ask* her?" Lexi asked me incredulously.

"I think it would be the right thing to do," I said.

"Look, either come or don't come," Lexi snapped.

"I'll let you know on Monday, okay?" I asked her.

"Okay," she agreed, and I could tell by the tone in her voice that she was certain I would come. "Oh, and be sure to wear something really cute," Lexi added. "There'll be high school guys there. Bye!"

I hung up the phone and just sat there a minute. Lexi Stanton had invited me to one of her parties. She thought I was cute. She thought I might be Gold material!

And then I got mad at myself. Since when was I so superficial that I cared what the in crowd thought? That wasn't like me at all. And as for the Gold Girls, Cindy, Tina Wu, and I had our own club. We hung out at the hospital and did things with the little kids. We had a purpose, a mission, and we were best friends, too.

So why was I sitting there, my heart beating triple time, just because Lexi Stanton had called me?

I didn't even like Lexi Stanton. She was a total snob. And she was mean to a lot of kids just because she didn't like the way they looked.

There was no way I was going to succumb to her flattery, or go to a party at her house when Cindy wasn't invited. And of course Tina wasn't invited, because Lexi didn't even know Tina.

I didn't care about Lexi or what she thought or her ridiculous Gold Girls.

I walked over to the mirror and looked at my reflection. Then I lifted my hand up to the mirror.

And even though I am ashamed to admit it, I was picturing what my little finger would look like with a narrow band of gold.

Chapter 3

"**M**ystery meat, again." Cindy sighed, as she looked with disdain at the dish of Hope Middle School cafeteria food she'd just picked up from the line.

"Maybe it won't taste as bad as it did on Friday," I ventured as I spooned a small bite of mixed vegetables into my mouth. I made a face at the taste.

It was Monday. Cindy and I had just had advanced-placement English together, and Ms. Ferrill had just given us another one of her impossible assignments: we were supposed to read a play of our own choosing by Friday and give a brief oral report to the class.

"Yeah, right," Cindy cracked. "It's worse." Then she took a small bite of the same vegetables and made a gagging noise at the same time.

"If you hold your nose while you chew, you won't taste it," I said. "You can't taste if you can't smell."

"Where'd you hear that?" Cindy asked me.

"I read it in one of my mother's medical books," I explained. "Sometimes I read my mother's medical books for fun. I find them interesting."

"Very weird, Veronica," she teased.

"It was for a report," I told her with dignity.

"Who wants to eat holding their nose, anyway?" Cindy asked me. "You hold your own nose. I'm not eating it." She pushed the plate away from her and pulled a candy bar out of her back pocket. "Emergency rations," she explained.

I looked down at the meat loaf and vegetables on my plate again. Too disgusting. I pushed it away.

"I can't believe we have to read a play," Cindy said. "You're supposed to watch plays, not read them."

"I like plays," I said. This was true. When I was living in New York, my parents used to take me to the theater quite often.

Of course, this was when they were still speaking to each other.

And now that I think back on it, half the time my mother got stuck at the hospital and I went with my father. Sometimes we gave my mother's ticket away at the last minute.

"I like plays, too," Cindy said. "Well, I like the one play I saw. Last year, Dad took us to see *Cats* at this huge theater in Detroit."

"That is not a play," I told her. "It's a spectacle."

"So, you tell me a good play to read, then," Cindy said. "Just make sure it's a really, really short one."

"Okay," I said, but my mind wasn't really on plays. I picked up my fork and mushed it around in the mashed potatoes. I had to tell Cindy about Lexi's party. I just had to. And it wasn't like me to hide something, or to beat around the bush. I am a very straightforward person. Usually.

But somehow this time I just couldn't bring myself to say the words.

"Hi, Veronica!" a voice came from behind me. I turned to see who it was.

Lexi Stanton. She was dressed in a gold T-shirt, a short, swirly gold and white skirt, and really cute white over-the-knee socks.

"Hi, Lexi," I said.

"So?" Lexi asked, flipping her perfect hair back over her shoulders. She was staring straight at me and totally ignoring Cindy.

"So what?" I responded, even though I knew exactly what she meant. I snuck a quick glance at Cindy, who had a puzzled look on her face.

"So..." Lexi said, meaningfully, as if to say, Are you coming to my party, or not?

"So, I don't know yet," I said.

"Oh, really," she said with a sigh. "I didn't know it was such a *monstrous* decision. Gawd!" She walked away and joined a group of Gold Girls at a nearby table.

Was Lexi mad at me? Was I really making too big a deal out of deciding whether or not to go to her party?

"What was *that* all about?" Cindy asked me, once Lexi was gone.

"Oh, nothing," I said evasively.

"It's not nothing," Cindy replied, taking a sip of the apple juice she'd bought. "Lexi Stanton doesn't talk to anyone new unless she wants something."

"That's probably true," I agreed. I cleared

my throat. Then I just sat there like an idiot.

"Spill it, Veronica," Cindy insisted.

Finally I just said it. "Lexi called me over the weekend," I said, "and invited me to a party on Saturday."

"Oh," Cindy answered, her voice quiet. And then, after a long pause, she added, "Are you going?"

"I told her I wanted to talk to you, first," I said honestly. "Because she wasn't inviting you."

"How do you know?" Cindy asked.

"I asked her; she told me," I replied.

"Oh," she said again. She was quiet for a moment. "Not that I'm surprised or anything. It's not like she's ever given me the time of day."

"I won't go if you'll feel bad about it," I said quickly. "I mean—"

"Do you want to go?" Cindy asked me.

I felt so guilty. I knew I shouldn't want to go. Only I did want to go. Only I didn't want to admit I wanted to go.

"I'm not sure," I finally said. "I don't particularly like Lexi..." That much was true.

"But she's supposed to give the coolest parties on the planet," Cindy filled in for me.

"Right," I admitted. "But I really will not go if you don't want me to go."

Cindy laughed. "What am I, your keeper? You should do what you want to do."

I frowned at her. "Are you sure?"

"Hey, we're not Siamese twins," Cindy said. "We don't have to go everywhere together."

I noticed how bright her voice was. Too bright, if you know what I mean. Like she was trying too hard to convince me. Like she really was hurt, but she just didn't want to admit it.

But I didn't let myself hear all that. I only paid attention to her words.

"Well, if you're sure..."

"Sure I'm sure," Cindy said. "I'll hang with Tina. No prob! Have a blast!"

I got the weirdest feeling. I knew that Lexi had treated Cindy really badly, and I knew that the right thing to do was not to go to the party.

But in my mind, I was already going through my closet, picking the perfect thing to wear to Lexi Stanton's party.

"Are you ready for your ballet class?" Miss Jenkins asked me as she came into the kitchen. She had just finished serving me dinner—I was eating alone, per usual, with just the television as company.

My mother was still at the hospital. My mother is *always* at the hospital.

"Yes," I said to her.

"Dr. Langley said I was to drive you to your class," Miss Jenkins said, jingling the keys to her car as she spoke. Miss Jenkins always calls my mother Dr. Langley, even though she has been working for us forever. And my mother never asked her to call her Patricia, her first name.

And *no* one, not even my grandparents, ever calls my mother "Pat."

I patted my dance bag, which was at my feet. "I'm ready," I told her.

"So let's go," Miss Jenkins said.

All the way to dance class, I thought about Lexi's party. I still hadn't told her officially that I was coming. But I knew I was about to see her in ballet class.

And I knew I had to tell her yes or no.

I knew I probably should say no, even though Cindy said it was okay to go.

But I wanted to say yes.

After Miss Jenkins dropped me off, I went into the main studio and pulled some extra leg warmers on over my leotard for my warm-ups. I started to stretch my leg muscles out, watching myself in the floor-to-ceiling mirror.

Which is how I saw Lexi Stanton come up from behind me, a big grin on her face.

"So," she said, dropping down to the floor next to me and starting her own stretching routine. "Have you tortured yourself enough over this momentous decision yet?" she teased.

I took a deep breath. This was my last chance to say no.

But "I'd love to come to your party" is what came out of my mouth.

"Cool," Lexi said as she gathered her hair up in a bun for class. "I knew you wouldn't turn me down."

"I was wondering," I said, as I lifted my right leg to the barre to stretch my muscles. "Maybe Cindy could come, and another friend of mine I think you'd like whose name is Tina..."

Lexi gave me a look like I'd just suggested she eat a full plate of cafeteria meat loaf and vegetables—without holding her nose.

"Are you *kidding*?" she asked me. And then she started to laugh. Clearly, she thought I was kidding, which I was not.

"I really would like them—"

"Cindy and whatever-her-name-is aren't coming," Lexi said dismissively. "But I'll tell you who is coming."

"Who?" I asked her, glancing up at the clock on the wall. Our actual class was starting in just a couple of minutes.

"Pete Worth," she said smugly, "who's on the football team at Hope High."

I'd never heard of him.

"Chris Lakewood," she continued, "who goes to Hope High. He is sooooo fine."

I'd never heard of him, either.

"And Trevor Wayne," Lexi said. "You know him. I've seen you talking to him at school."

"Trevor Wayne?" I repeated in shock. Trevor was extremely cute and very popular, but I had never known him to hang out with Lexi and her friends.

"Ha!" Lexi cried, then her voice dropped to a whisper. "I knew you liked him. Here's your big chance."

I gulped. Cindy had a huge crush on Trevor Wayne. They had been buds forever, but Cindy desperately wanted Trevor to see her as a Girl with a capital *G*, and not just as a friend, if you know what I mean.

And lately it had seemed to me that things were definitely moving in that direction. Trevor had gotten to be good friends with my cousin Brad, and both Trevor and Brad hung out with us at the hospital a lot when we were doing things with the little kids.

And now Trevor was going to Lexi's party. Without Cindy.

What was even worse was that Trevor had kind of flirted with me when I first moved to Hope, but as soon as I found out Cindy liked him, I didn't respond to him at all, except as a friend.

Cindy knew that. Kind of. But when it came to Trevor, she felt really insecure. And when she found out I was going to Lexi's party and Trevor was going to Lexi's party and she was not invited, she was going to be really, really hurt.

"Listen, Lexi," I said, lifting my leg from the barre. "Cindy really likes him."

Lexi rolled her eyes. "Some girls like Brad Pitt," she said, "but that doesn't mean they have a chance with him."

"But...Trevor likes her, too," I said.

"Not enough to stop him from coming to my party," Lexi said smugly. "And he never asked if he could bring her, I might add."

"Maybe he's going to," I said feebly.

"I doubt it," Lexi said. She held onto the

barre and dropped into a graceful plié. "Anyway, I heard he likes you, not Cindy. So you should be thanking me. I'm doing you a favor."

"But Cindy Winters—"

"Listen, Veronica," Lexi said, her voice turning cold. "I don't want to hear about *Cindy Winters* anymore. You want to spend Saturday night with *Cindy Winters*, go right ahead. Don't come."

Just then the bell in the studio chimed, indicating that class was about to start.

"It's going to be a blast!" Lexi said, her voice happy again. "And I'm really, really glad you're coming. See ya!" Lexi walked away from me and over to where her stuff was, about twenty feet away.

I stood up, turning to where Miss Faye had come into the studio, the whole situation going around and around in my head.

I was going to be at Lexi's party. So was Trevor. Cindy wasn't invited.

And I was going to have to tell Cindy that Trevor was going to be there before she found out from someone else.

CHAPTER 4

"I'm going home!" Heidi cried as I entered her hospital room Tuesday afternoon. She was dressed in a new pink dress—pink is Heidi's absolute favorite color—and the short blond hair that had grown back in after her brain surgery was tied with a slender pink ribbon.

Cindy, her sixteen-year-old brother, Clark, and her dad, Dan Winters, were all crowded around Heidi's bed. "Doesn't Heidi look gorgeous?" Cindy asked, her eyes shining with happiness for her little sister.

"Perfect," I agreed.

I noticed that Cindy looked really cute,

too. She had on a pink sweatshirt—in honor of Heidi, of course—and some new black jeans with pink stitching around the pockets. I felt guilty just looking at her smiling face. I hadn't told her about Trevor going to Lexi's party yet. And even though I knew it wasn't my fault that Trevor and I were invited and she wasn't, I felt responsible, anyway.

"Cute outfit," Cindy said casually, since she was not a person who tended to dress up. In fact she usually wore baggy jeans, and she had a hard time keeping all the buttons on her shirts. I looked down at my pale pink leggings, pink ballet slippers, and delicate white sweater with a pink lace collar and cuffs. It had cost a fortune at some boutique on Madison Avenue in New York, and it was one of my favorite outfits. But I would have gladly given the outfit away rather than have to tell Cindy about Trevor.

Well, I couldn't think about that now. I had to concentrate on Heidi and her party. We had all put a lot of time and effort into planning it, and I wanted it to be perfect as much as Cindy and Tina did.

"Cindy, could I talk to you for a minute?" I asked.

"Sure," Cindy said, and we walked into the hall. As soon as we got out of sight, Cindy's attitude changed completely. "So, is everything ready?"

"Everything," I confirmed. "Everything" was the surprise farewell party we had planned for Heidi. The theme was "Think Pink." Tina and I had rushed over after school to decorate the children's playroom with pink and white crepe paper, pink and white balloons, and a huge banner made by all the kids that read WE LOVE YOU, HEIDI! The staff had made another banner that read THINK PINK! in huge neon pink letters. Rachel Dander, a pediatric nurse who was secretly dating Cindy's dad, had baked a cake with pink frosting. Some of the other nurses and social workers had made food, too—there were pink frosted cookies, pink marshmallows, and pink cupcakes.

My mother, who had taken care of Heidi, had come up with perhaps the best pink food of all. She had rented a cotton candy machine that made pink cotton candy, along with a girl dressed in a pink uniform who would spin them out as long as the kids kept eating them.

How nice of her, how wonderful, how

caring. I knew that's what everyone would say. But spending money is nothing to my mother. It's not like she took time to actually bake something, like Rachel or Virginia or the others. My mother had never baked anything in her life.

All she did was make a phone call and give them her credit card number. Big deal.

"Everyone is waiting in the lounge," I reported. "Tina has all the kids organized. They wanted to start eating all the pink food, but she made them wait."

"Good," Cindy said. She squeezed my hands. "I am so excited," she told me. "Sometimes I thought this day would never come."

Cindy kind of blamed herself for Heidi's accident, since she had been with Heidi on the Ferris wheel. Not that it was Cindy's fault. The safety bar broke—that's how Heidi fell. But Cindy had been paying more attention to me and Trevor—we had been walking through the amusement park together—than she had to her little sister.

That made me feel kind of guilty, too.

Not that there was anything going on with me and Trevor. I had gone to that amusement park by myself, and I just happened to run into him there. But Cindy thought that Trevor liked me, and now we were both invited to Lexi's party, and...

I had to stop thinking about it. Or I would never make it through Heidi's party.

"Let's get Heidi," I said eagerly.

Cindy peered at me. "Is something wrong?"

"No," I said quickly. "Why would you think that?"

Cindy shrugged. "You had the weirdest look on your face just now."

"It's nothing," I lied. "Let's just get Heidi to her party."

"It's show time!" Cindy agreed happily, and we went back into Heidi's room.

"You ready for a ride, Princess?" Dr. Dan asked, holding the wheelchair close to the bed. Dr. Dan is the name the kids call Cindy and Heidi's dad. He isn't really a doctor, though.

"I don't want to go in a wheelchair!" Heidi exclaimed. "I'm better now!"

"It's a hospital rule, Heidi," Clark said patiently.

"No, I don't want to," Heidi pouted.

I couldn't blame her. After all the time in the hospital, she wanted to leave on her own two feet.

"Hey, sometimes rules were meant to be broken," Dr. Dan said with a shrug. That's the kind of guy he is—happy-go-lucky, easygoing, fun to be with. Can you imagine having a father that wonderful?

Dr. Dan reached out his arm for his little girl. "May I escort you out, Your Highness?" he asked her.

Giggling, Heidi took her father's arm. We all followed behind her, Clark carrying her little suitcase. When we got into the hall, Heidi looked all around, and then looked up at her father. "No one is here."

"I guess they're in their rooms," Dr. Dan said.

"But...I thought maybe my friends would want to say goodbye to me," Heidi said, her bottom lip quivering.

"Maybe some of them are in the playroom," Cindy suggested casually. "Want to go see?"

"Okay," Heidi agreed.

We all walked down the hall to the playroom, Heidi and her dad leading the way. As soon as Dr. Dan opened the double doors, everyone yelled, "Surprise!"

Those that could jump up and down jumped. Everyone clapped their hands and hooted and hollered. Nurse Rachel Dander, who has long blond hair, huge blue eyes, and is sickeningly sweet, jumped the highest of all.

"Surprise, surprise, surprise!" she yelled. "Oh, I love surprises!"

"Oh!" Heidi exclaimed, and put her hands to her cheeks. She looked up at her father. "Is it for me, really?"

"Really, Princess," he assured her, reaching down to give her a hug.

"Do you think all your friends would let you leave without a party?" Cindy asked, hugging her little sister.

Everyone talked and laughed at once, and a whole crowd of people gathered around Heidi. They all had pink construction-paper hearts that read WE LOVE HEIDI pinned to their shirts. Many of them had presents, which they piled on the long table, next to the pink cake.

"I'm gonna miss that girl," Jerome told me as he hopped over to me. I noticed he had his crutches wrapped with pink crepe paper for the occasion.

"But you're glad she's going home, aren't you?" I asked him.

"Now, what do you think, woman?" Jerome asked gruffly.

"Dumb question," I conceded. "Are you sure you aren't really a thirty-year-old man trapped in a ten year old's body?"

"I ask myself that same question all the

time," Jerome said with a dramatic sigh. "Later." He smoothly hopped away on his crutches.

"Everybody!" Rachel cried, clapping her hands together. "Let's all watch Heidi open her presents! Won't that be super fun?"

"Yeahhhhh!" the little kids yelled, and everyone crowded around the table. Heidi sat on a high chair someone had thought-fully produced. She really was like a queen surrounded by her court.

"I'll throw some magic fairy dust on Heidi so all the presents are exactly what she wants!" Rachel cried. She reached her hand into the pocket of her uniform and threw some shimmery dust into the air. The littlest kids oohed and aahed. One of the older kids who had been there awhile stuck her finger down her throat and rolled her eyes.

"Help, I'm in sugar shock just watching her," Tina said, sidling over to me. She looked extremely darling in hot pink overalls over a white T-shirt covered with pink hearts.

"Ditto," Cindy agreed, walking over to us as she ate a pink-frosted cookie.

"Oh, well, Heidi loves her," I pointed out.

"So does someone else," Tina said

significantly. She cocked her head toward Dr. Dan, who was beaming at Rachel.

"Oh, gag me!" Cindy cried. "My father is not-not-not in love with Tinker Bell!"

We call Rachel Tinker Bell because she walks around on her tippy-toes and she actually wears a Tinker Bell costume sometimes, to entertain the little kids.

"Look at how he's looking at her," Tina said. "It's mad, passionate love!"

"You have a vivid imagination," I said dryly.

"When it comes to romance, I, Tina Wu, know all and see all," Tina said in a worldly voice.

"When it comes to romance, you, Tina Wu, are crazy," Cindy corrected.

"A new Barbie!" Heidi squealed, as she opened another present. "Oh, thank you!"

"I happen to be the oracle of romance," Tina said smugly. "Which one of us has a boyfriend?"

"You," Cindy allowed. "But I don't want one."

"You would if it was Trevor," Tina pointed out.

Trevor. There it was again. I was going to have to tell her that he was invited to Lexi's party. But how?

"You know, Veronica, I still think we should fix your mom up with Cindy's dad," Tina said, folding her arms.

"Please don't start on that again," I warned her.

"It's a crazy idea," Cindy agreed.

"Well, don't blame me when you end up with Tink as your stepmother," Tina said with a shrug.

"You are truly out of your mind, Tina Wu," Cindy said, shaking her head.

All three of us looked across the play-room. Just at that moment, Rachel said something to Dr. Dan that we couldn't hear. He laughed and put his arm around her shoulders, and gave her a quick hug.

"Ah-ha!" Tina exclaimed triumphantly. "Today hugging, tomorrow...who knows?"

Cindy's face went pale. "I have to have a talk with him."

"Before it's too late," Tina added significantly. She gave me a casual look. "Your mom isn't dating anyone, right?"

"You know my parents aren't even divorced yet," I said. My voice sounded colder than I had intended. "I think they're probably going to get back together," I added without thinking.

Now, why had I said that? Nothing either

of them said or did would lead me to that conclusion.

"I didn't know that!" Tina exclaimed.

"Did your mom say something?" Cindy asked eagerly.

"Not exactly," I admitted. "Forget I said anything."

"But it's so romantic!" Tina exclaimed. "Love lost, found once again..."

"How do we put up with her?" Cindy asked me with a laugh.

"You love me and you know it," Tina said with a big grin. "Hey, I'm dying for one of those pink cupcakes. You guys want me to get you one?"

"No, thanks," I said.

"Later," Cindy said.

"I may have to eat two or three," Tina said with relish as she headed for the long table of food.

I looked over at Heidi. She was still opening her presents, with all the kids and staff gathered around her. Now was my chance to talk to Cindy. I took a deep breath. "Cindy?"

"Look how happy she looks," Cindy said, gazing at her little sister.

"I need to talk to you," I said firmly.

She tore her eyes away from Heidi, who

was opening a huge box tied with pink ribbon. "What?" she asked me.

"It's about Lexi's party," I began.

"Oh, that?" Cindy asked, a smile on her face. "I told you, I don't care about that. I mean it, it's no biggie."

"Trevor's going," I blurted out.

The smile fell from her lips. "Trevor?"

"I didn't have anything to do with it," I said quickly. "Lexi told me at ballet last night that she had invited him."

"Maybe he's not going," Cindy said.

"I guess he already told her he would. That's what Lexi said, anyway."

Cindy was quiet for a moment. "Well, I can't really blame him. I mean, her parties are supposed to be so rad and everything."

"Cindy—"

"And you know Trevor and I are just buds—"

"Cindy—"

"So it's really okay," she said, her voice getting that too-bright sound again. "It's not a problem."

"I know you feel badly," I said. "I know how much you like him."

"Yeah, well, I guess that feeling isn't exactly mutual," she said, still trying to sound up-beat. "So if you want to go for him—"

"I told you I would never do that!" I exclaimed.

"I know he likes you," she said.

"He likes you, too," I said feebly.

"Yeah, like a sister," she said. "I was stupid to think it was anything more than that. Like he's going to fall for an ironing board."

She was referring to the fact that she really didn't have much of a figure yet. I hated when she put herself down like that.

"You know how cute you are," I said earnestly.

"Oh sure," Cindy said. "I know. But he doesn't."

She gave me a funny look. I knew what she was thinking. Veronica the Perfect. That's what she called me sometimes. And it was so utterly, totally not true.

"Maybe Trevor will invite you," I said tentatively.

"Yeah, right," she snorted. "The only people who go to Lexi Stanton's parties are invited by Lexi Stanton, and everyone knows it."

"Look, Cindy, I don't have to go—"

"I want you to go, I told you!" Cindy insisted. "It's just a party, you know. It's not the end of the world. Now, let's go help Heidi cut her cake, okay?"

Right. Not the end of the world. Just a party. One stupid little party. Not really very important at all.

That's what I kept telling myself as I tried to ignore the hurt behind Cindy's too-bright smile.

CHAPTER 5

I looked at myself in the full-length mirror on the back of my closet door and frowned.

"Totally wrong," I said, pulling off the fifth outfit I had tried on. I went back to pawing through my closet.

It was Saturday night, and I was getting ready for Lexi Stanton's party. I had already tried on everything from a Betsey Johnson black leather minidress to ripped jeans, and absolutely nothing felt right.

"I can't look like I'm trying too hard," I mumbled to myself as I pulled a simple yellow and white babydoll dress out of my closet. It had spaghetti straps, so I pulled a little white lace T-shirt out of my drawer to wear underneath it. I put the whole outfit on and checked out my reflection again.

"Decent," I decided. I put on the smallest amount of brown mascara and some cherry-flavored lip gloss. Then I threw my head upside down and brushed my hair until it crackled with electricity. I weaved a tiny braid on the right side and tied it at the end with a tiny yellow ribbon. Then I surveyed my reflection again. Well, it would have to do.

There was a knock on my door. I knew it had to be Miss Jenkins, who was driving me to the party.

"I'll be right out, Miss Jenkins," I called to her, quickly spraying my neck and wrists with some vanilla-scented perfume.

"It's your mother," came my mother's proper voice.

My mother. She must have gotten home while I was getting dressed.

"Hi," I said, opening the door for her.

"You look lovely," she told me as she came into my room. She sat down at the chair in front of my desk and smoothly crossed her long legs.

"Thank you," I said. "I'm going to a party." I pushed tiny pearl studs through my pierced ears and popped the backs on.

"Yes, you mentioned it to me a few nights ago," she said.

I had. She had actually been home for dinner one night, so I went through the charade of asking if I could go to this party Saturday night, which was being given by a girl in my class.

"Will it be chaperoned?" she had asked me as she sipped a crystal glass of sparkling water.

"Of course," I told her, which from what I had heard about Lexi Stanton's parties was pretty much a lie.

"You know I trust you, Veronica," my mother had said. "Use your own judgment."

"Okay," I had said.

"Miss Jenkins will take you there and make sure the party is adequately chaperoned," my mother had continued, "and she will pick you up again at precisely eleven o'clock."

"But everyone stays later than that...."

"This is not open to negotiation," my mother had said, picking up her fork again.

And that, as they say, had been that.

"So, you're home," I said lamely, since I couldn't think of anything else to say to her. It was pathetic, really. When I thought about all the times I had wished she was around, wished that I could really talk to her, and now that she was actually here, I had nothing to say.

"Yes," my mother said. "I...wanted to talk to you." She reached into the pocket of her perfectly cut Armani jacket and brought out a letter.

I recognized the handwriting on the envelope. It was from my father.

"I haven't got much time," I said, quickly looking at my watch. For some reason, I felt nervous. Whatever it was, I had a feeling I didn't want to hear it.

"Sit down, Veronica," my mother said.

I sat down on the bed.

"I got this letter from your father today," she told me, slapping the letter against the palm of her left hand.

"You could say your husband," I pointed out. "He is still your husband."

She ignored that. "He sent me some... interesting news," she said. "It seems he has moved."

"He sold our apartment?" I asked incredulously. We had a huge, incredible apartment on the Upper West Side of Manhattan, overlooking Central Park.

"It's on the market," she explained. "It

seems he...is living elsewhere."

"Where?" I asked, totally bewildered. "He couldn't find a better apartment."

"That's true," my mother said. "He is living in a house. On Long Island. He's commuting."

"Daddy bought a house?" It all just seemed too bizarre.

"No, he didn't buy a house," my mother said slowly. She looked down at the letter and slapped it against her palm again. "It seems that he has been seeing a woman— she's a lawyer—for quite some time now. And he moved in with her. Into her house."

I just sat there for a minute. I couldn't believe it. "That can't be true," I finally said.

"That's what his letter tells me," my mother said stiffly.

"But...he would never do that without telling me!" I cried.

She didn't say anything.

"But...how long could he possibly have been seeing her?" I asked. "It's not like we left a year ago." And then I had a terrible thought. "Was he with this woman while you were still together?" I asked my mother in a hushed voice.

"I don't really know," she said, getting up.

"Anyway, I felt that I had to tell you, Veronica. I'm sorry that he didn't tell you himself."

I gulped hard. "Maybe he wrote me a letter before he wrote to you, and it got lost in the mail."

"I sincerely doubt that," my mother said. "It won't do you any good to hold on to fantasies about him, Veronica—"

"I'm not!" I cried. "I'm just...never mind. Just never mind."

She stood at the door. "For whatever it's worth," she said quietly, "I'm sorry he hurt you." Then she walked out and softly closed the door behind her.

"Hi, Veronica, come on in," Lexi said, opening the front door to her huge house. She only lived a few blocks away from me, in a redbrick Colonial with shutters painted pale blue.

All the way to her house I had vowed to myself that I would not think about my father. Or my mother. Or about how scared and angry I felt. And hurt. How could he do that to me, just move out of our apartment and move in with some strange woman, and not even tell me about it?

Well, I just wouldn't care, that's all. I

vowed to put him out of my mind and just have fun.

"Nice wheels," Lexi said, looking at our BMW.

I looked back at Miss Jenkins, who was still waiting in the BMW in front of Lexi's house. I waved to her, and thankfully she drove away. So much for my mother's insisting that Miss Jenkins check on the "chaperon."

"Your mom?" Lexi asked, amusement playing around the corners of her mouth.

"A friend," I mumbled, since I really didn't want to explain.

I quickly took in what Lexi was wearing— a black cashmere sweater with such a wide neckline that it fell off one bare shoulder, and black leggings. On her feet she wore perfect little gold flats, which of course matched her perfect little gold pinky ring. She looked like she was eighteen years old, at least.

"Everyone is in there," she said, cocking her head toward the family room.

"Thanks," I said, and I walked toward the party while she greeted two boys I didn't know.

"Hi, Veronica!" said a girl I barely knew as she ran over to me.

"It's...Abbie, right?" I asked her, thinking fast. She had only started at Hope Middle School the week before. She was in my algebra class.

"Right, Abbie Messinger!" the girl said. She was slender, with shaggy red hair, and really beautiful green eyes. She was wearing faded jeans and a sheer white embroidered blouse, through which you could see her pretty lacey white bra.

"Have you been here long?" I asked politely, looking around at the party. There were already about thirty kids milling around the huge family room. I didn't see Trevor. I recognized the Gold Girls from school, plus some guys from our grade and from ninth grade. Some of the other kids there looked much older. The large-screen TV was tuned into MTV, and the volume was cranked up loud. At the moment, a Green Day video was on.

"I got here about fifteen minutes ago," Abbie said over the music. "I've been, like, totally freaking out with nerves, ya know?"

"It's just a party," I said, trying to sound casual.

"Oh, come on, it's Lexi Stanton's party!" Abbie said. "I've only been in Hope a week, and even I know what that means!"

"What?" I said.

"She is everything!" Abbie cried. "I mean, look at her!" I looked into the front hall, where Lexi was laughing with two cute guys who looked like they were in high school.

"No one is everything," I said sharply.

"There's someone like her at every school," Abbie said, still looking at Lexi, who now had her arms wrapped around one guy's neck. "At my old school in Toledo, her name was Alisha. She had her own gang, called the Nasty Girls."

"The Nasty Girls?" I repeated with distaste.

Abbie shrugged. "It's a much tougher neighborhood than this is. Lots of gangs. One kid got shot in my school. Anyway, you had to get jumped into the Nasty Girls."

"What's that?" I asked.

"You know, where every girl in the gang gets to beat you up, and you have to take it and remain standing," Abbie explained.

"But...that's terrible!" I exclaimed. "That's crazy!"

"Well, like I said, it's much tougher there. That's why my parents finally moved away. Anyway, I was too scared to get jumped. So I never got to join."

"Maybe you were just smart," I suggested. Something caught my eye in the front hall. Trevor had just arrived. And Lexi was hugging him.

"I was so excited when Lexi invited me to this party," Abbie confided. "Do you know what she said to me? She said I might be Gold Girl material!"

"She told me that, too," I admitted.

"She did?" Abbie asked. "That's fantastic! That means we can both get in together!" Then she furrowed her brow. "You don't think we'd have to get jumped in, do you?"

"Of course not," I snapped. Lexi still had her arms draped around Trevor. "Excuse me," I said. "I...have to use the ladies room." I was making that up. But I did not intend to spend the entire party listening to Abbie Messinger tell me about her life.

"It's that way," Abbie said, cocking her head across the room. "I ran in there when I first got here, I was so nervous."

"Thanks," I said, and I weaved my way through the crowd toward the bathroom.

"Oh, hi, Veronica," a girl called to me. It was Dawn McKnight, a cheerleader from school. Dawn was best friends with Krystal Franklin, who had been in a terrible car accident that had scarred her face. Krystal was out of the hospital, but she still hadn't come back to school. Frankly, neither Dawn nor Krystal was a very nice person.

"Hello," I said, and headed for the bathroom.

I locked the door and stared at my face in the mirror. I looked okay. Normal. No zits. Clear eyes. Pretty hair. Everything was going all right. So why was I so nervous?

I washed my hands, brushed my hair, and popped a breath mint, then I took a deep breath and headed back into the party.

Now some kids were dancing. Including Trevor, who was dancing with none other than Dawn McKnight. Slow dancing. He had his arms wrapped around her waist, and she had her arms wrapped around his neck.

"Dance?" a guy asked, coming over to me. He was tall, almost six feet would be my guess, with dirty blond hair and deep-set blue eyes.

"Okay," I agreed, and moved into his arms. Fortunately he didn't pull me too close.

"I'm Chris," he said, "Chris Lakewood."

Chris Lakewood! Lexi had mentioned him! He went to Hope High. And Lexi thought he was gorgeous. Well, actually, I did, too.

"I'm Veronica Langley," I told him, as we moved slowly to a ballad by Counting Crows.

"Oh, yeah, Lexi mentioned you," Chris said. "You just moved here or something."

"From New York," I explained.

"No kidding?" Chris asked. "Wow, I've always wanted to go there. So, you in eighth?"

I nodded.

"I'm a sophomore," he said. He looked down at me. "You think I'm too old for you?"

"Oh, no!" I said quickly. Then I felt like an idiot. "I mean, I don't even know you, but you can't be that much older than I am. That's what I meant."

Chris laughed. "Lexi's friends are always wild," he said. "Know what I mean?"

"Sure," I agreed, even though I didn't have a clue.

The song finished, but Chris kept his arms around me. "So, you want a beer?"

I admit it, I was shocked. I had never tasted a beer in my life, and I had never been to a party where there was beer before. Okay, call me socially retarded. But all I could think was that my mother would kill me. And I wondered where Lexi's parents were.

"No, thanks," I said, trying to sound casual.

"Okay, well, I'm gonna get one," Chris said.

"Lexi's parents let her serve *beer*?" I blurted out.

Chris laughed. "Lexi's parents are very cool. They never interfere in her life. The beer, though, is out in my buddy's car. Her parents don't know about it."

"Oh," was all I could think of to say.

"So, you sure you don't want to come outside with me and pop a brew?"

"No, thanks," I said. "I'll wait here."

"I'll be back for you," he promised. And he walked away through the crowd.

I wandered over to a long table in the corner where there were soft drinks and paper cups, and I poured myself a Coke. I leaned against the table and looked around. Someone had turned the lights down low. I noticed that all the Gold Girls were wearing some subtle item of clothing that was gold. For Lexi, it was her gold flats. A gorgeous girl named Amanda had a peace symbol on a slender gold ribbon around her neck.

Heather Thompson wore a gold sweater that dipped to a deep *V* in the back. *What would it be like to be one of them,* I wondered, *so perfectly confident at all times?*

I bet that none of them had a father who dumped his family for some woman with a house on Long Island.

And even if they did, I bet they were so cool that they didn't care.

Some kids were in the dark corners kissing. Abbie was with some guy with a crew cut, sucking face. How could she? I mean, she had to have just met him!

"Hey, there," Trevor said, coming over to me. "I didn't know you were coming to this party." He poured himself a Coke and took a huge gulp. "Man, it's hot in here." He turned to me. "Having fun?"

"It's all right," I said carefully. "It would be more fun if Cindy and Tina were here."

"Well, Lexi doesn't even know Tina," Trevor said, throwing back some more Coke. "And I'd bet any amount of money that Cindy can't stand Lexi Stanton."

"Or the other way around," I said pointedly.

"Hey, you know Cin," Trevor said. "You know the mouth she has on her. Believe me, she can't stand Lexi."

"But you can," I said sharply.

Trevor shrugged. "She's okay," he said. "She gives great parties."

"How could you?" I blurted out.

"What?" he asked me, looking at me as if I was crazy.

"How could you come to this party without Cindy?"

"What does Cindy have to do with anything?" Trevor asked.

I brushed some hair off my face. "You know how much she likes you, Trevor," I said.

"I like her, too," Trevor said. "She's one of my all-time favorite people."

"I mean she *likes* you–likes you," I said pointedly.

"Well, I kind of like her like that, too," Trevor said.

"Really?" I asked hopefully. "Then why—"

"Hey, hold on," Trevor interrupted. "Cindy and I have been buds for years. So it's kind of weird, okay? Things are changing with us..."

"But that's good!" I exclaimed.

"Well, it doesn't just happen overnight, you know," Trevor said gruffly. "We're not, like, going steady or anything."

"I know," I admitted. "But—"

"So just back off," he said sharply. "Did Cindy put you up to this?"

"Oh, no, I swear she didn't!" I said, grabbing his arm. "Please, don't tell her I even said anything to you. She would hate me!"

"I won't," Trevor said. "Hey, I'm sorry I bit your head off. Listen, this is just a party. It's not a big thing. And Cindy is cool. I mean, she's special, ya know?"

"Yes, I do," I agreed fervently. "I'm sorry I was so rude to you..."

Trevor laughed. "You are the most proper girl I ever met, you know that?"

I sighed. "I've been told that before."

"Hey, don't steal my girl," Chris said, walking back over to us.

His girl? Did he mean *me*?

"Trevor was just about to dance with me," Lexi said, walking over to us and wrapping her arms around Trevor's neck. "Weren't you?"

"Sure," Trevor said. "Excuse us."

"And you were just going to dance with me, right?" Chris said, smiling a heart-meltingly gorgeous smile at me.

"Yes," I agreed. "I was."

He took me in his arms. And this time he held me close. And it felt good. So what if

I didn't even know him. I could get to know him. He was gorgeous and cool, and he seemed to like me.

And when I was in his arms, I didn't think about my parents at all.

CHAPTER 6

"**H**ey, Veronica, hurry up!" Lexi's voice echoed irritably through the girl's restroom at the Hope County Centre Mall. "I'm not spending all day in here with you."

"I'll be right out," I called back from inside the bathroom stall.

"I love your hair like that, Lexi," I heard Abbie Messinger say.

"Thanks," Lexi said. "I bought this stuff that's supposed to add shine."

"Well, it worked!" Abbie said eagerly. "You'll have to tell me what it's called so I can get some!"

I hated the way Abbie sounded, so

pathetically eager to suck up to Lexi. But I don't sound anything like that, I assured myself.

"Uh, Veronica!" Lexi called to me again. "Sometime this year, okay?"

I flushed the toilet and fumbled with the snaps on my bodysuit, then I looked quickly at my watch—it was three o'clock in the afternoon. I did some very fast mental calculations.

It was the day after Lexi's party. Lexi had called me that morning to see whether I wanted to go to the mall with her and Abbie. I said yes right away. I mean, Lexi could call any one of the Gold Girls, but she had called me. And Abbie. I wasn't so sure I liked Abbie all that much. She just seemed so *desperate* to me.

Lexi's mom had brought us to the mall at around one. I had asked Miss Jenkins to pick me up at the mall at three-thirty, because I was supposed to meet Cindy and Tina at Hope Hospital at four. An eight-year-old girl named Marissa Ruiz, who had been a patient for a long time, was coming back in for some follow-up tests. Marissa had been badly burned in a fire. We had all come to love her, and we were really eager to see how much she had improved since she left the hospital.

I knew it would take about a half hour to get to the hospital, and since I had promised to meet Cindy and Tina there at four, everything should work out perfectly.

When I heard about girls going to the mall together just to hang out, I had always thought it sounded incredibly stupid. Back in New York City, we don't even have any malls. Everyone in Hope went to the Hope County Mall, but I hadn't been there yet. Tina's parents—or should I say her grandmother—would never let her go hang out at the mall, and Cindy never had any money. And what free time the three of us had, we usually spent at the hospital.

But now I had to admit that hanging out at the mall with two other girls had been really fun. We'd tried on clothes at three or four different stores, just for fun. Lexi had bought a cute skirt at The Gap, and Abbie bought some earrings that were on sale at an inexpensive jewelry store. We tried on all the different body oils at the All Natural Store, and then we went to a new boutique called X that Lexi told me had just opened. The clothes in there were fantastic and very expensive. I tried on an incredible outfit—matching miniskirt and vest in hand-crocheted lace. Lexi and Abbie both said it looked great on me. Well, I have my own credit card, compliments of my mother. I don't use it all that much. But I took it out and bought the outfit as if it was something I did every day. I could see that Lexi was impressed. And I had felt both good and bad.

Good that I had impressed her, and bad that I cared.

I finally got my bodysuit snapped and came out of the stall.

"It's about time," Lexi said, as I washed my hands. She handed me my outfit from X, which was hung on a perfect pink satin hanger and then wrapped in plastic with the X logo. "We need to hit the food court."

"I am totally starving," Abbie said, as we quickly walked to the area where all the fast food stands were located.

"Not me," Lexi said. "I'm on a diet."

"Oh, me too," Abbie agreed. "I am, like, so totally fat!"

I looked at her. She wasn't fat at all.

We got in line at the Italian Station and bought slices of pizza and Diet Cokes, then we took them over to one of the few empty tables.

We hadn't been sitting there for two

minutes when three guys came over to the table and sat down. Two of them I had never seen before. The third one was Chris Lakewood.

He looked even cuter than he had at Lexi's party, if that was possible. He had on worn jeans and a light blue and white checked flannel shirt. The blue in his shirt matched his eyes.

"Don't eat that, you'll get fat," a dark-haired guy said to Lexi. He picked up her pizza and took a huge bite.

"You cretin!" Lexi cried, grabbing for the pizza, but I could tell she really wasn't mad at all.

"Hi," Chris said, pulling up a chair next to me. "Long-time-no-see."

"Hello," I said politely.

Chris laughed. "Are you always like this?"

"Like what?" I asked.

"So formal," he said, making a face. "Loosen up or something!"

I blushed and patted my mouth with my napkin. I couldn't help the way I was. It was how I was raised.

"This is Andy," Chris said, nodding at the dark-haired guy, "and this is Burt."

"Hi!" Abbie said eagerly. "I'm Abbie! Anyone want to share my pizza?"

"I'm not even speaking to you guys," Lexi told Chris's friends. "You didn't come to my party last night."

"We went to a keg party at E.M.U.," Burt said, reaching for Abbie's Coke without even asking her. "I got totally wasted."

I sipped my Coke and looked at him out of the corner of my eye while he talked about the party. I knew that E.M.U. had to be Eastern Michigan University. So they had been at a college party!

"I borrowed my old lady's car," Burt was saying. "I practically totalled it coming home."

If he borrowed his mother's car, that meant he was at least sixteen. Sixteen! As old as Cindy's brother, who treated us as if we were in kindergarten.

"Burt and Andy go to H.C.C.C.," Lexi said significantly.

"H.C.C.C?" I responded. "What's H.C.C.C?"

"Veronica just moved here, from New York," Lexi said quickly to the guys.

"Fast City," Andy said, raising his eyebrows at me.

"H.C.C.C. is Hope County Community College, right?" Abbie asked.

"Abbie's new, too," Lexi said in a patronizing voice.

"Let me tell you, college is great," Andy said. "No one cares if you show up or not!"

"It's a lot harder than high school, though," Burt added.

"Oh, I really feel for you!" Chris said with a laugh. "I can't wait to get to college!"

I couldn't believe Chris's friends. They were actually in college! College! Which meant they were at least eighteen. So what were they doing hanging out with girls in the eighth grade?

"So how's Erica?" Burt asked as he polished off Lexi's pizza.

"She's okay," Lexi said. "She said the guys at U. of M. are to-die-for." She turned to me. "These bozos went to high school with my older sister," she explained.

Oh, so *that's* what was going on!

"Of course, it's really me they were always after," Lexi added snottily.

"Listen to her!" Andy hooted, and tickled Lexi in the ribs. She pretended to fight with him and finally ended up sitting on his lap with her arms around his neck, like it was the most normal, casual thing in the world.

"Hey, I'm lonely!" Burt pouted, looking at Abbie.

"Aw, I'll make you feel better!" Abbie said quickly, and she popped into his lap.

Chris looked at me and put his hands out. I just sat there, playing with my straw.

"Oo, Chris, shut out!" Andy hooted.

I could feel my face turning as red as the ugly plastic chair I was sitting on.

"Hey," Burt said, "the new Jim Carrey movie starts at five-twenty in the multiplex. You girls want to go? With us?"

"We'll pay," Andy added.

"Oh, big spender," Lexi teased. "I am *so* impressed."

Abbie looked at Lexi, waiting to see whether she would go or not.

"Hey, I'll throw in a popcorn," Andy said with a grin.

"Oh, well, in that case, how can I refuse?" Lexi said, tossing her hair off her face.

"I can go, too," Abbie agreed, giving her hair the same toss.

Everyone looked at me.

"That's not for a really long time," I finally said. "I'll have to leave before that."

"What are you talking about?" Lexi said. "That's in, like, twenty minutes!"

"What are you talking about?" I said, looking at my watch. I had just checked it and knew it was a little past three-thirty.

Which is exactly what time my watch said when I looked at it again.

My watch had stopped, somehow. It wasn't three-thirty, it was five o'clock. Which meant that I was really, really late.

Oh no.

"I have to go," I said, my voice a little frantic as I gathered up my purse and my outfit from X.

"Was it something I said?" Chris asked in a teasing voice.

"You are a total loser with girls, my man," Burt teased him.

"Where are you going?" Lexi asked me.

"I'm so late!" I called back as I was already practically running for the mall entrance.

"Call me!" Lexi commanded, her voice reaching me over the din of the mall.

I bolted for the main doors. Sure enough, Miss Jenkins's car was parked right outside, the motor running, and she was inside, reading a copy of a tabloid.

"You're late," Miss Jenkins said as I pounded frantically on the locked passenger-side door.

"I know," I said, quickly getting inside. "Why didn't you come looking for me?"

Miss Jenkins pulled the car away from the curb and steered it toward the parking lot exit. "Would you really have wanted me to come in there and embarrass you in front of your friends?" she asked as she pulled out of the lot onto the highway leading back to Hope.

When we got to the hospital, it was already five forty-five. We'd hit a bad traffic jam on the way there.

"Please wait here," I said to Miss Jenkins as she dropped me by the front entrance. I knew I was in big trouble with my friends for being so late.

"I'll wait over there," Miss Jenkins said, pointing to an empty parking place nearby.

I jumped from the car and ran up the interior hospital stairs to the pediatrics wing, praying that Cindy and Tina would still be there.

The first person I saw when I came out of the stairwell was Jerome, who was patrolling the hallway on his crutches.

"You may be fine, but you're also late," he said to me accusingly.

"Are Tina and Cindy still here?" I asked him hopefully.

"No," he said emphatically. "Marissa's appointment got changed to next week. Cindy and Tina hung out and waited for you, but you didn't show. They just left."

"Oh no," I said, shaking my head. "It wasn't my fault!"

"Somebody hold you up?" Jerome asked me. "'Cause if they did, I'll get my homies to ice him." He propped himself up on his left crutch, made a shooting motion with his right hand, and then blew imaginary smoke away.

"No," I said with a sigh, leaning back against the wall.

"You messed up, then," Jerome said, turning away and continuing on down the hall.

I felt terrible. Slowly I walked over to the elevator, pushed the down button, and rode the elevator back to the ground floor. And wordlessly I got into the car and let Miss Jenkins drive me home.

"Your mother's home," Miss Jenkins said as we pulled into our driveway.

"That's nice," I said, not knowing what else to say.

I let myself in through the garage door and walked upstairs, passing my mother in her study. The first thing I wanted to do was call Tina and Cindy and apologize for missing our time at the hospital.

"Veronica?" a voice called out. "Is that you?"

My mother.

I turned and went into her study, where

she was sitting, typing some kind of a report into the computer. "It's me, Mom," I said.

"Were you at the hospital?" she asked me, a little distractedly.

"I got there late," I said quickly.

"Oh," my mother said, her eyes on the computer screen.

"Were you on the ward?" I asked.

"Rounds," my mother intoned. "Miss Jenkins will have dinner ready for us at eight." She began to type on the computer keyboard again.

Not a question from my mother about why I was late. Not a question about who I was with. Not a question about the party last night.

There's no one I can talk to except for Tina and Cindy, I thought. *And I let them down today.*

In my room, I quickly dialed Cindy's number. I was going to tell her the truth.

"Yeah?" Cindy's brother, Clark, answered the phone.

"Hello," I said. "It's Veronica. May I please speak to Cindy?"

"Veronica!" Clark said. "Are you okay?"

"I'm fine," I said in shock. Clark never made conversation with me. "Why?"

"Cindy told us you didn't make it to the

hospital," Clark said. "She tried to call you, but there was no one home."

"I'm sorry, I just...didn't make it," I said lamely.

"Look," Clark told me, "she's out with Heidi and Dad. But I'll tell her you called. Okay?"

"Okay," I said. And then Clark hung up.

I dialed Tina's number. Her grandmother answered.

"Hel-lo?" she said briskly. "Who this?"

"This is Veronica Langley," I said. "May I please speak to Tina?"

"Tina Wu busy now," Tina's grandmother pronounced. "No disturb. She doing home-work."

"But it will only take a moment," I pleaded. "It's really important."

"What school you go?" Tina's grand-mother asked.

"Hope Middle," I said to her.

"Public school?" Tina's grandmother demanded.

"Yes, it is," I said.

"You do homework yet?" Tina's grand-mother asked me.

"I've finished it already," I told her, which was true. I did it in the morning, right after I woke up.

"Ha!" Tina's grandmother said. "You no get enough homework. That why Tina Wu no attend public school. She busy. Do homework now. You call tomorrow. Goodbye."

And then she hung up. And I did, too.

I sat back on my bed. I really needed someone to talk to. But I couldn't talk to my mother, because she wouldn't talk to me. And I couldn't talk to my father, who was busy with some woman on Long Island whom I had never even met. And I couldn't talk to my best friends, because one was busy with her sister and her dad, and the other was doing her homework, which would be checked by her mother because her mother was her teacher.

And even though my mother was home, it felt like I was all alone, and I could hear the beating of my own heart.

CHAPTER 7

"I'm really sorry, my watch stopped," I told Tina and Cindy for the zillionth time.

It was the next day after school, and we were all in the playroom at the hospital. We had just finished reading stories to the younger kids, who were now gathered on the other side of the room watching cartoons on TV.

"Veronica, we said it's okay," Cindy told me.

"We know you weren't late on purpose," Tina added. "And anyway, Marissa didn't even come in."

"So, was it fun going shopping with Lexi?"

Cindy asked with exaggerated casualness.

"It was okay," I said.

"Who is she?" Tina asked, idly picking up a crayon. She began to color in one of the coloring books the kids had left on the table.

"She's the most popular girl at our school," Cindy reported. She gave me a quick look. "And she's not exactly the nicest thing on two legs."

I couldn't disagree with Cindy. What she had said was true.

"I saw that guy again," I told my friends.

"A guy?" Tina asked, looking up from her coloring with interest. "What guy?"

"I met a guy at Lexi's party," I explained. "I already told Cindy about him. His name is Chris Lakewood. He goes to Hope High."

"How old is he?" Tina asked.

I shrugged. "I don't know. He's a sophomore."

"Wow, he must be at least fifteen!" Tina said, wide-eyed. "Is he cute? Is he nice? Are you going out with him? Tell me every detail!"

"There's not much to tell," I admitted. "He was at the mall yesterday with his friends. We met them at the food court. He tried to get me to sit on his lap."

"So did you?" Tina asked breathlessly.

"No," I snapped. "I don't even know him! I can't stand girls who act like that!"

"Then why are you suddenly hanging out with girls who act like that?" Cindy asked.

"All I did was go to the mall with her once," I mumbled guiltily.

Tina picked up a purple crayon and began to color a bunny's ears in the coloring book. "Can you imagine what my grandmother would do if she ever caught me sitting on a boy's lap? I'd never be allowed out of the house again!"

"My father thinks I'm still a baby," Cindy said with disgust. "If he caught me sitting on a guy's lap, it wouldn't faze him a bit. He'd just think I was cute!"

"Wait till I tell you guys what my grandmother did to my sister Sherry when she didn't do her homework," Tina said. She launched into a long story, which Cindy followed with some story about Heidi.

I just sat there, listening. I don't have any brothers or sisters, so I had nothing to add. *What would it be like,* I wondered, *to actually have a big family?* People who cared about me, people to fight with, even.

I would never know.

* * *

"Hello, Dad?" I said, holding the cordless phone tightly in my hand. "It's me!"

It was a couple of hours later, right before Miss Jenkins was going to serve dinner. My mother wasn't home. I had decided to call my father, to give him a chance to tell me about...well, whatever there was to tell me about.

I had given it a lot of thought. And it occurred to me that maybe he had been afraid to call me, maybe he was afraid that I'd be mad at him. The more I thought about it, the more that made sense to me. That had to be it! Well, I would just call him and let him know that I wasn't going to reject him or anything just because he was living with some strange woman. I dialed the new phone number my mother had given me, and he answered the phone.

"Oh, hi, Veronica," he said. His voice sounded funny, I thought. Guarded. Careful.

"So, you moved!" I said brightly.

"Yes, I did," he acknowledged. Silence. "So, how's everything? How's school?"

"Oh, it's great," I told him. "I'm getting mostly straight A's. I got a B in algebra."

"Well, you can bring that up," he said. "Work harder."

"I will," I promised. "So, what's new?"

I waited for him to tell me, to explain everything, but silence greeted my question.

"Dad? Are you still there?" I asked.

"Just a sec, Veronica," he said. I could hear him talking to someone else in the room. "My daughter," I heard him say. Someone else—a woman—said dinner was ready. He told her he'd be off the phone soon. "I'm back," he finally said to me. "We were just about to sit down to dinner."

"Oh, well, we don't have to talk long," I replied.

"How's ballet?" he asked me. "Have you found a good teacher?"

"Miss Faye, she's decent," I told him. "Not like New York, but decent."

"Well, good, honey," my father said.

"So...I heard you're living with someone," I commented casually.

"Yes," my father admitted. "She's...a friend."

"Well, I guess she's more than a friend if you're living with her," I said, my voice sounding sharp in my own ears.

"A good friend," he amended.

"So are you marrying her or something?" I asked.

"Veronica, please—" my father said in a warning voice.

"It wouldn't even be legal, you know," I told him. "Your divorce isn't even final from Mom yet."

"Veronica—"

"I'm kind of surprised you haven't even mentioned this 'good friend' to me," I continued. "I mean, I am your daughter."

"There really isn't anything to tell," my father said stiffly.

"There isn't?" I asked, my voice rising. I began pacing with the phone in my hand. "You're living with her and there's nothing to tell me?"

"Veronica, calm down," my father said.

"I don't want to calm down!" I cried. "Why didn't you even tell me about her?" This was not the way I had planned this conversation at all. But I couldn't seem to control myself.

"Veronica, please," my father said. "Don't get upset. There is absolutely nothing for you to get upset about. Don't make a scene."

Somehow when he said that, I felt even angrier than I had felt before. "I'm not making a scene!" I screamed.

"Look, Veronica," my father said in a steely voice. "My love life has nothing to do with you. I am an adult. And your mother and I have separated. What I do with my personal life is none of your business."

I felt as if someone had punched me in the stomach. None of my business. Tears came to my eyes. I was in so much pain, I couldn't even open my mouth.

"Veronica? Honey? Look, that didn't come out the way I meant it to. I only meant that I deserve some privacy, I'm sure you can understand that. Honey? Are you still there?"

"I'm here," I managed, wiping the tears from my cheeks with the back of my hand. "You're right. I'm acting like a child. You can have all the privacy you want."

"Thanks, honey," my father said. "Thanks for understanding."

"Hey, Martin!" I heard a young female voice call to my father.

"I'll be off the phone in a minute, Kitty," my father said.

"Can you help me with my science homework?" the voice asked. "I am totally confused."

"After dinner," my father called to her.

"You're living with a woman who has

science homework?" I asked, aghast. "What is she, a college student?"

"That was Kitty, my friend's daughter," my father explained in a tense voice.

"Her daughter," I said dully.

"She's fourteen," my father said. He was quiet a moment, then his voice sped up really fast. "She's a really nice girl. You'd like her. When you come out to visit me the two of you can get to know each other."

"Sure," I said. "Well, I have to go now. Goodbye." I hung up the phone.

And then I just sat there. My father was living with a woman who had a fourteen-year-old daughter named Kitty. Just one big happy family.

So now I knew the truth. Why he hadn't called me.

He had replaced more than Mom. He had replaced me, too.

"Chris Lakewood likes you," Lexi informed me as we warmed up at the barre for ballet class two hours later.

"So?" I asked, gracefully swinging my arm over my head to stretch my waist.

"So he's only the cutest sophomore at Hope High," she said, fixing the back of her ballet slipper. "He's never gone after an eighth-grader before."

I shrugged and turned to the barre, where I began to do pliés.

Lexi gave me an appraising look. "Well, I'm impressed. Aren't you the cool one?"

I shrugged again. I wasn't about to tell her that I had more on my mind than Chris Lakewood. Like my father. And some fourteen-year-old girl on Long Island named Kitty.

"We could double sometime," Lexi suggested. "You and Chris and me and Andy. Andy has his own car."

"Chris never even asked me for my phone number," I pointed out, fitting a stray hair back into my bun.

"Well, he's been asking me about you," Lexi reported. "I think the four of us could have a blast together."

"Your parents don't mind if you go out with a guy who's in college?" I asked her.

"Oh, I just tell them we're hanging out like friends," she said. "They know Andy from when he used to hang with my sister, so they buy that." She laughed. "It's a good thing they haven't seen the hickeys he's been giving me!" She lifted her chin up. "Can you tell? I covered them with make-up."

"I can't see anything," I told her honestly.

"So, you want to double sometime? I told Chris I'd ask you," Lexi said.

"Sure," I said as if I could care less. It was weird, really. I didn't even like Chris, but I liked that he liked me. And although I had been kissed, I was very, very far from experienced, but I acted like Lexi's story about dating a college guy and getting hickeys was the most ho-hum thing in the world. I felt like I was outside watching myself, like I didn't even know who I really was anymore.

"You're really cool, Veronica," Lexi told me, giving me another of her appraising looks.

"Thanks," I said, and I began to do a few arabesques.

"You know, I was thinking," Lexi said, leaning close to me. "Friday night we're having a Gold Girls' meeting at my house. I'd like you to come."

I put my leg down and looked at her in the mirror. "Really?"

"Sure," Lexi said. "I really do think you might be Gold Girl material. So, do you want to come?"

Did I want to be a Gold Girl? Did I want to become part of the most popular crowd at school, dress like they dressed, go where they went? Well, did I?

Maybe. I had never been in the in crowd before. Wouldn't it be fun to be among the coolest of the cool? Wouldn't the attention and envy be better than the terrible emptiness I felt?

But what about Cindy? And Tina? Maybe once I was a Gold Girl, I could get Lexi to invite Cindy and Tina, too. It wasn't impossible.

"I'll think about it," I told her.

She gave me a look of renewed respect. It was as if because I wasn't jumping all over her, she liked me better.

"Let me know," she said coolly. Then she smiled a smug smile. "Although I already know exactly how you'll decide."

CHAPTER 8

"This meeting of the Gold Girls will come to order," Lexi commanded.

The other seven girls in her family room immediately stopped talking and stared at her expectantly. It was Friday night, and there I was, at my first meeting of the Gold Girls.

All week I had tried to bring it up to Cindy, but she was out of school, home with the flu, and I just couldn't see telling her about it on the phone. Her father said I couldn't visit her because she was contagious. I wanted to go over to Tina's, but her grandmother was on the warpath because Tina had flunked one of her mother's history tests and almost flunked a math test. She had been spending so much time on the phone talking with Brad that she hadn't been studying. She wasn't allowed to go out all week, not even to the hospital, and she wasn't allowed to have any friends over, either.

There was no one else I could talk to. My father called twice, but both times Miss Jenkins answered the phone, and I told her to tell him I wasn't home. What could we possibly have to say to each other? He had made his position pretty clear—his life was none of my business. Well, I figured that meant my life was none of his business, either.

On Thursday my mother came into my room and just sat there, as if she wanted to talk to me. I thought about telling her about it then. But she looked so uncomfortable, and she just asked me all these stiff questions about how school was going, and how ballet was going, and I knew that the whole thing was useless.

I had absolutely no one to confide in. Not even a pet. So I had called Lexi Thursday night and told her I was coming to the meeting. I could tell that she was impressed that I'd waited until the very last night to say I was coming. She mentioned that Abbie Messinger would be there, too; that we were both being considered for membership.

"But just between you and me," Lexi had confided to me, "I don't think she has much of a chance."

As Lexi talked about some party they had all gone to, I looked around at the group. They were all pretty, all rich and confident, all incredibly cool. They all wore something gold, and they all had those little gold rings on their pinky fingers. They all belonged.

Except for me and Abbie. Abbie sat forward on Lexi's couch, hanging on every word Lexi said. I noticed that she had on jeans and a narrow gold belt, with a tiny ribbed gold sweater that bared her stomach. I hadn't worn gold at all. After all, I wasn't one of them yet. I had on black velvet jeans, black ballet flats, and a conservatively cropped pale pink angora sweater. Around my neck I wore a black velvet ribbon with a tiny diamond tear that hung right between my collar bones.

"Before we get to new business," Lexi said with a superior smile, "I have great news. Something came in the mail today."

"The jackets?" Heather asked with excitement. "I thought we weren't getting them until next week!"

"My dad arranged it priority," Lexi said. She got up and went to a nearby closet and pulled out a huge box.

Everyone started talking at once as they pulled the box open. Inside were gold satin baseball jackets, with each girl's name embroidered over her heart. They all put their jackets on, everyone except Abbie and me.

"That is so rad," Abbie said enviously.

"I love them!" Amanda Ricky cried, looking down at her name on her jacket.

"We can wear them to the Michigan game next weekend," Julie added.

"We're going to Ann Arbor to a football game," Amanda explained to me and Abbie. "With a bunch of guys from Hope High."

"Oh, now we can get our Glamour shots done!" Julie added. "We'll all get our shots taken in our jackets, okay?"

"I think we should check and see if Glamour will do a group one of us," Dawn suggested.

"Thank your dad for getting the jackets so fast for us, okay?" Heather said, pulling her hair out from under the jacket's collar.

"You know he'd do anything for Lexi," Julie said. "He thinks she walks on water."

"Well, I do!" Lexi said with a laugh. Everyone laughed with her. She settled back in her oversized chair, adjusting her jacket around her. "So," she said. "There are a couple more jackets in the box." She looked significantly at Abbie and then at me.

Abbie's jaw dropped open and she stared at the box covetously. Did Lexi mean there were jackets in there for me and Abbie? Had they already agreed that we should be Gold Girls, too?

"As you guys know, we're looking at two possible new members tonight." She carelessly pushed her hair back with two fingers. "Abbie Messinger and Veronica Langley."

Abbie beamed at everyone in the group; they all stared back at her coolly. I just sat there.

"We don't take new members very often," Lexi continued.

"And we might not take any now," her friend Julie Monroe added sharply. Julie had long chestnut brown hair—even longer than mine—and huge green eyes. Cindy had told me she had been voted Best-Looking in seventh grade, and she and Lexi had had a huge fight over it.

"First, you should know what it means to be a Gold Girl," Lexi said, her face serious. "We are always there for each other, no matter what. We're family."

The heads around her nodded in agreement.

"We come first for each other," Julie continued. "Before anyone or anything. Understand?"

Abbie and I both nodded.

"I think you two should tell us why you think you're Gold Girls material," Lexi said, sitting back and crossing her legs. "You first, Abbie."

Abbie took a deep breath. "Well, I, uh...really admire you guys," she said, biting her lower lip. "I mean, you guys are everything, you know?"

"Oh, we know!" Dawn McKnight said with a laugh. "But that doesn't tell us why *you* should be."

Abbie looked panicked. I could see sweat break out on her brow. "Well, I'm cute—at least that's what guys tell me," she said with an ingratiating grin. "I'm loyal to my friends, no matter what."

Some of the girls nodded at that, which clearly made Abbie feel better.

"I love to party!" Abbie continued. "And I like to get wild! I mean, if you guys like to get wild. And...I'm not afraid of anything!"

"Oh, really?" Lexi asked coolly. She traded a meaningful look with Julie Monroe. I had no idea what it signified.

"What about you, Veronica?" Lexi asked, turning to me. "Why are you Gold Girls material?"

"I have no idea," I said. I was not going to sell myself to them. I had watched Abbie do it, and it was too pathetic for words.

"Well, I for one am not impressed with your I'm-too-cool-for-you-because-I'm-from-New-York act," Dawn McKnight said sharply.

"I'm not putting on an act," I said quietly. "And I don't think I'm too cool for anyone."

"Evidently not," Heather Thompson said. "Look who she hangs out with."

"What's with you and Cindy Winters?" Julie asked.

"She's my best friend," I said in a low voice.

"There's no accounting for taste," Dawn said with a laugh.

"Cindy Winters is okay," Lexi pronounced.

"Please!" Julie snorted.

"I said she's okay," Lexi said sharply.

That gave me hope. Maybe if I got in, Lexi really *would* invite Cindy!

"Well, what about that other girl you hang out with at Hope Hospital?" Dawn asked. "Deena or something? Some Chinese girl?"

Dawn had met Tina when she and her best friend, Krystal Franklin, had gone to a charity carnival at Hope Hospital. Krystal had been really mean to Tina. And after Krystal's car accident, when she was in the hospital, Tina, Cindy, and I had often seen Dawn visiting her friend. In fact Krystal had been a Gold Girl, too. But that was before. Before her face was ruined. Before she left Hope to go live with relatives in Connecticut, where, I had heard, she was having plastic surgery on her face.

"Her name is Tina Wu," I explained. "And she's as American as you are."

"Oh, well, *excuse me*," Dawn said snottily.

"Look, we're not voting on Veronica's friends," Lexi said with exasperation. "We're voting on Veronica."

"A girl is known by the company she keeps," Heather pointed out.

"Well, if she becomes a Gold Girl, she'll be

keeping new company, won't she?" Lexi pointed out. That shut Heather up immediately. Lexi looked at Abbie, then at me. "Every girl here had to pass an initiation to get into the Gold Girls," she said.

Abbie's face paled. I remembered what she had told me about girls in her old neighborhood getting "jumped" into a gang. But I didn't think it could be that.

"We all stole something at the mall that was worth over a hundred dollars," Julie explained.

"Oh, cool!" Abbie said eagerly.

As for me, I was shocked. I had never stolen anything in my life. Were they going to ask me to steal, too? I would say no, I decided. Absolutely. But then I'd never be a Gold Girl. Well, so what? I looked around at the circle of friends in their gold baseball jackets. They all belonged to each other. They were a part of something. With all my heart, I wanted to be a part of something, too.

But would I steal for it?

"The whole stealing thing is getting boring," Julie said. "We've come up with something much better for you two."

"Just tell us what it is!" Abbie said eagerly.

103

"It can't be something easy," Heather warned. "You understand that."

"Sure," Abbie agreed. She looked over at me. I nodded.

"Well, here's what we decided you have to do to prove you should be one of us," Lexi said, leaning forward. "Do you know the old abandoned house out on Nottingham Road?"

I nodded. Everyone knew about that house. It was on a narrow road on the outskirts of Hope, a big white house with badly peeling paint. It sat on top of a huge hill. Everyone said the house was haunted. Cindy had told me that years ago a girl had been murdered in that house, and no one had lived in it since.

"You mean the haunted house?" Abbie asked, her face white. Evidently she had heard about the house, too. "Is it true that a girl was murdered there?"

"Six years ago," Julie said. "The house belonged to the Peegram family. Allissa Peegram was twelve years old. Someone came in through the window and murdered her in her sleep. The crime was never solved."

"And after that the family moved away," Heather added.

"It's the only murder we've ever had in Hope," Julie said in a hushed voice.

I shuddered and wrapped my arms around myself.

"Everyone knows the house is haunted," Lexi said. "Even the guys are afraid to go in that house."

"A couple of years ago some guys from Hope High went there drinking," Julie said. "They saw the ghost of Allissa, and she, like, attacked them!"

Everyone in the room was quiet, just imagining that.

"But those guys are wusses," Lexi said, looking straight at Abbie. "You aren't afraid of anything. Isn't that what you said?"

"R-right," Abbie stammered.

"Good," Lexi said smugly. "Here's what you and Veronica have to do to get into the Gold Girls. You have to spend the night, tomorrow night, in that house."

"*Sleep* there?" Abbie asked in horror.

"Sleep there," Lexi confirmed. "And just to make sure you actually do go in, yesterday Julie and I hid something gold in the house, and you have to bring it back to us. You're not going to be able to go to some hotel and lie to us afterward."

"You weren't scared to go in?" Heather

asked. Evidently the others didn't know that Lexi and Julie had been inside the house.

Lexi gave Heather a cool look. "Do I look like I was scared?" She turned to Abbie. "So, what do you think?"

"I—I—" Abbie stammered.

"If you're too scared, just forget it," Julie snapped at her.

Lexi reached down into the box at her feet and slowly pulled out a gold jacket with the name *Abbie* embroidered on it. Then she pulled out another jacket, with my name embroidered on it. "It's not hard to remove your names, you know," she said.

I admit it, I wanted that jacket.

I wanted to go to college football games wearing that jacket that matched all my friends' jackets. And spending the night in an abandoned house didn't seem nearly as terrible to me as stealing. Besides, I didn't really believe in ghosts.

"I'll do it," I said decisively.

Everyone turned to look at me. They were clearly surprised that I said yes so easily.

"I knew it," Lexi said with a triumphant grin. She turned to Abbie.

"I will, too," Abbie said, even though she sounded scared to death. "It's no biggie, right?"

"Right," Lexi agreed. "You can tell your parents you're spending the night at my house. Naturally I'll cover for you. All the Gold Girls will be spending the night here. At dawn, the two of you are to come back here with the gold item from the house. Got it?"

"Got it," I said, and I gave Lexi as cool a look as she was giving me.

"Sure!" Abbie agreed, even though her mouth was twitching with nerves.

So, I had decided. I was going to pass the test to be a Gold Girl. Then I would get one of the jackets, and the little gold ring. My life would be full and happy and exciting. I wouldn't even have time to think about my mother. Or my father. Or how scared I was that I was losing my father forever. I'd be a Gold Girl.

And Gold Girls weren't afraid of anything.

CHAPTER 9

"I'm not so certain I want to do this," I said softly, taking a long, slow look at the Peegram house.

"Me neither," Abbie said.

The ramshackle white house, barely visible in the dim quarter-moon light, loomed up ahead of us on the hill. It looked lonely. And dark.

And very, very scary. It seemed like the kind of place where someone would get murdered.

Where someone actually *had* been murdered.

It was the next night. I'd told my mother

that I was spending the night at Lexi's, and Miss Jenkins had actually dropped me off at her house. All the Gold Girls were there, planning everything for their Glamour shots at the mall the following weekend. Fifteen minutes later, after Abbie's mother dropped her off, the two of us had walked, our sleeping bags in hand, the three miles out of town to the Peegram house.

We'd followed Lexi's directions exactly, walking on Old Calumet Road north until a dirt road forked off it. Then we followed the dirt road until it dead-ended.

It was a really strange walk.

I had absolutely nothing to say to Abbie. She was nervous, and she kept going on and on about how wonderful it was going to be to be a Gold Girl, and how she wanted it more than she'd ever wanted anything in her life. I felt badly for her, I really did. But I had absolutely nothing to say to her.

I couldn't help thinking how different it was from when Cindy and Tina and I were together. There was so much to say, so much to do. Well, there had been, anyway. Lately things seemed to be changing for us. Now that Heidi was home, Cindy was busier helping to take care of her. And Tina's family was so strict, it seemed like they barely let her out of the house. They were both so busy with their families, it felt as if they didn't really have time for me.

But the Gold Girls had time. They were more important to each other than their families, that's what they had said. They were always there for each other. Well, that's what I wanted.

But did I want it badly enough to sleep in that house, where a girl had been murdered?

"This is crazy," I murmured, still staring at the house. At that moment, I would rather have been anywhere than at the bottom of the hill, looking up to that house on the hilltop. It hadn't seemed so terrible the night before—certainly better than stealing—but now that I was standing there with Abbie, looking at the house, it seemed like the craziest, scariest thing in the world.

"It's worth it, right?" Abbie asked fiercely.

I didn't answer her.

"Don't you want to be a Gold Girl?"

"Yes...I guess...I don't know," I said honestly.

It was very dark. And very quiet. The only thing I could hear was the cheep-cheep of a few crickets that had managed to survive the early autumn frost a couple of weeks ago. We'd passed the last streetlight when we turned off the paved roadway.

"What do you mean, you don't know?" Abbie cried, shifting her sleeping bag from under her left arm to under her right. "How can you not know? Do you know how many girls would kill to be a Gold Girl?"

"I just don't want to die to be one," I said, still staring at the house. Even though I'd dressed warmly, in jeans, a sweater, a big hooded sweatshirt, and hiking boots, suddenly I was feeling very, very cold.

"I'm going in," Abbie finally said, "even if you're not."

But I could tell Abbie was just as nervous and as scared as she'd been the night before, because neither of us made any kind of a move to approach the house.

Off in the distance, some kind of animal howled mournfully.

"What was that?" Abbie asked, grabbing my arm tight.

"Just a bird or something," I said. "An owl, maybe."

"I never heard an owl that sounded like that."

"Look, we don't have to do this," I said. "We can walk back to my house. I'll just tell my mother we changed our plans."

"Won't she think that's weird?" Abbie asked.

"No, she won't even pay any attention," I said truthfully.

"Veronica," Abbie said, her voice full of false bravado, "I'm not scared. Not at all."

"Yes, you are," I said.

"No, I'm not," Abbie repeated.

And with that, Abbie started to take purposeful strides toward the old house. Helplessly, I started to follow her. What choice did I have? I couldn't let her go in there alone. And I sure didn't want her telling Lexi Stanton that I was too afraid to go into an abandoned old house.

Slowly, cautiously, the two of us climbed up on the porch.

"Do you believe in ghosts?" Abbie asked me. I thought I could hear her teeth chattering a little.

"No," I said.

"But don't you think it's possible?" Abbie demanded. "I mean, it's possible, right?"

"Ghosts are a figment of the imagination," I said firmly. "They don't exist." I took a deep breath and walked purposefully over to the front door and tried it.

Locked.

"How did Lexi and Julie get in?" Abbie wondered.

"A window," I guessed, looking around.

"Let's try this one," Abbie said to me, pointing to a window to the left of the door.

I went over to it and gave a push on the sash.

Nothing. I tried it again. This time, there seemed to be a little movement.

"Maybe if we push together," I suggested.

"Okay," Abbie said, taking hold of the left side of the window. We both gave a quick upward push, and the window flew open.

Abbie and I looked at each other. Then, defiantly, Abbie started to climb in.

"Watch out for snakes," I said, cautioning her about something that I remembered reading.

"What?" she yelped, one leg in the window and one leg out.

"Snakes," I repeated. "I read in one of my mother's medical textbooks that poisonous rattlesnakes like to go inside warm places. That's why I wore boots."

"Thanks for warning me ahead of time," Abbie hissed, looking down at her sneakers.

"Just don't make any noise," I said. "Try to be quiet."

"I hate snakes," Abbie repeated fearfully. But to my great surprise, she pulled her left leg up and into the open window.

And I followed her.

Quietly, so quietly, the two of us started through the inside of the house. We'd both brought flashlights, and they lit the way. Earlier, we'd decided that the best thing to do would be to find the gold item Lexi and Julie had hidden, and then figure out what to do and where to sleep.

"Where do you think Lexi would hide it?" Abbie whispered to me.

"I think—"

"Sssh!" Abbie hushed me. She grabbed my arm in a death-grip.

"What is it?" I asked her, standing perfectly still.

And then I heard it.

Thump.

Thump thump.

"Did you hear that?" Abbie whispered, her voice totally petrified. If anything, she grabbed my arm even tighter.

"Yess-ss," I hissed back, quavering.

The two of us stood stock still, listening intently. But the noise seemed to have stopped.

"It must be the house settling," I said, gulping hard.

"Yeah," Abbie agreed, "whatever that means."

"Could you please let go of my arm?" I whispered to her. "You're cutting off the—"

Thump.

Thump thump. Thump thump thump thump.

"Oh my God, Veronica," Abbie hissed frantically, grabbing my arm again. "It's the ghost, it's the ghost!"

The two of us stood, frozen in our tracks, as the thumping grew louder.

"Who's there?" a growly male voice called. "Who's there? Who's in the house?"

Abbie screamed.

And then, I heard the loudest sound I'd ever heard in my life.

A blast. Like a gun going off.

Abbie screamed again.

"Oh my God," she cried. "Oh my God!" She fell to the floor.

"What is it?" I yelled, trying to focus my flashlight on her with my shaking fingers. "Abbie?"

"Who's there?" the male voice called again. "WHO'S IN THE HOUSE?"

I couldn't move, couldn't breathe. The light from a powerful flashlight fell on my face, blinding me. Then it moved from me to Abbie, who was still on the floor, crying and moaning.

"Oh, sweet Jesus!" the male voice exclaimed.

"Help me!" Abbie groaned, "Veronica, help me!"

"Oh, sweet Jesus, I've shot a kid!" the male voice cried.

He ran toward me, out of the darkness, the light still trained on Abbie. I screamed as loud as I could.

"Jesus," the man kept yelling. He knelt over Abbie. And that's when I saw it, when all the craziness started to make some sense.

There was blood gushing out of two holes in the leg of Abbie's jeans.

The man knelt over Abbie. He was about forty years old, and he had a long, full dark beard.

He was wearing pajamas.

He stood up quickly and turned on me.

"Don't shoot!" I begged. "Don't!"

He didn't say a word, he just knelt back down by Abbie and thrust his hands immediately over the bullet wounds in her right leg.

I felt the world spinning out of control, but I forced myself not to fall.

"Veronica! Help me!" Abbie cried again.

It had to be some horrible nightmare I was caught in. All of this couldn't possibly be real.

But it was.

In a split second, I understood what had happened. The Peegram house wasn't abandoned.

At least, it wasn't abandoned tonight.

Abbie and I had broken into it, and there was someone already inside. Someone who probably belonged there. We had surprised him. He thought we were burglars. And he'd shot Abbie, not knowing that the burglars were actually a couple of eighth-graders.

"We gotta get her to the hospital," the man said to me. "What the hell were you two doing in here?"

"It was—" I started to explain.

"Tell me later." He cut me off. He reached down and scooped Abbie up in his powerful arms. "What's the nearest hospital?"

"Hope Hospital," I said quickly.

"Let's go," he ordered. For a moment I didn't move, I was just rooted to the spot in horror. "Move!" he screamed at me as he carried Abbie toward the door.

Like an automaton, I followed him around the porch and behind the house, where he loaded Abbie into the backseat of an old Chevy.

An old Chevy we had never seen. If we had, we never would have gone into that house.

"You gotta help me, kid," the man said to me. "Keep your hands on her leg. And *press!*" I did as he told me, Abbie crying and moaning, twisting her head around, screaming.

"It'll be okay, Abbie," I told her, which is one of those stupid things people say when they know that nothing is really okay at all.

The man jumped into the front seat, started the car's engine, and tore out from behind the house and down the dirt road, toward Old Calumet Road.

"Which way do I turn?" he asked me frantically.

"Left!" I ordered him. "Left! Then go straight till you see the signs!"

"Oh God, God, please help me," Abbie said weakly. She had stopped screaming and thrashing around. She seemed to be growing weaker. There was blood everywhere. All over her leg, all over my hands, and even some on the car seat.

"You're going to be fine, Abbie," I assured her, trying to press harder on the holes in her leg. "We're almost at the hospital."

"Am I going to die?" she asked me weakly.

"No!" I insisted as her blood gushed over my hands. "You're not going to die!"

I closed my eyes and held my hands down on her leg, trying desperately to stop the bleeding. And then I prayed. And I didn't stop praying, even after we came to a stop outside the Emergency door of Hope General Hospital, and then followed behind as Abbie was loaded onto a stretcher and quickly whisked away.

Inside, the man fell back into one of the ugly plastic seats in the Emergency waiting area.

"Are you hurt?" a nurse asked us both quickly, looking at the blood that covered us.

"No," I said. I was barely holding it together.

"Those two kids broke into my house," the man said, wiping his hand across his face. "I thought they were burglars. I didn't mean to shoot that little girl. Oh, God... I didn't mean to hurt anyone..."

"I'd better call the police," the nurse said quickly, and she hurried off to use the phone behind her desk.

She dialed and spoke quickly, then hung up. "The police are on their way," she told us.

I walked over to the nurses' station. "Could I use the phone, please?"

"Sure," she said, moving it toward me. Her eyes were full of compassion. I quickly dialed my home phone number and stood there feeling numb as the phone rang.

"Hello?" came my mother's voice.

"It's me," I said, using all my willpower to control my voice.

"Veronica?" my mother asked. "Is everything okay?"

"No," I managed. And then it was like a dam burst inside of me, and tears gushed out of me as I doubled over, racked with sobs. "I'm at the hospital," I gulped out. "There's been a terrible accident. Come right away. Oh, Mommy!"

"I'll be right there," I heard my mother say as I slid to the floor, sobbing so hard I thought I would never, ever stop.

CHAPTER 10

"Try to eat something, Veronica," my mother said gently.

Eat? How could I eat? How could I ever do something as simple as eat food again?

It was early the next morning, and my mother and I were going to leave soon to go back to the hospital to see Abbie.

I had just called Lexi on the phone and explained what had happened the night before. She hadn't shown much of a reaction when I told her that Abbie had been shot.

Abbie. Abbie had been shot. It had really happened.

I closed my eyes, and the horrible events of the night before flashed through my mind once again.

The nurse had called Abbie's house, and her older brother had said that their mother was at a friend's, and he would call her and tell her to come to the hospital.

My mother had arrived only seconds before the police. She held my hand while I managed to choke out to them what had happened.

"We thought the house was deserted," I told them, tears running down my cheeks. "We never, ever would have gone in if we knew someone was there. We weren't going to take anything, it was just...just a stupid prank..."

The police wrote it all down in a little notebook, asking me some questions from time to time, their faces very serious. As I was giving my statement, the man who had been asleep in the house walked over to us.

"Is it your house these girls broke into, sir?" the blond-haired policeman asked. He had told me his name was Officer Paulson.

"My brother's," the man said. His face was terribly white against the blackness of his beard, and his light blue pajamas were stained with blood.

"Your name, sir?" the other cop asked politely. His name was Officer O'Rourke.

"Bob Peegram," the man said. "I just got to town last night. I'm meeting...I was supposed to be meeting with Hope Savings Bank today. My brother is putting the house on the market. He's never been able to come back after his daughter...after the tragedy with my niece. So I told him I'd come try to sell the house for him."

"Could we see some identification, sir?" Officer Paulson asked.

Mr. Peegram automatically felt where his pants pocket would be, but of course he had on pajamas. Pajamas covered with blood. "I don't have my wallet," he said. "I had to run out..."

"We understand, sir," Officer Paulson said. "Do you have ID in your car? A registration?"

Mr. Peegram went out to the car while I continued giving my statement to the other policeman. And all the time my mother just sat there, holding my hand.

Finally Mr. Peegram and Officer Paulson came back into the waiting room. Mr. Peegram looked over at me and shook his head. "This is a terrible tragedy," he said, his voice breaking. "It never should have happened. I never meant to..."

"I'm so sorry," I told him, fresh tears welling up in my eyes.

He didn't answer. He just put his head in his hands and sobbed.

I gave the police the rest of the story. They took it all down in their little book. Then they turned back to Mr. Peegram. "Under the circumstances, you're obviously not guilty of anything. Do you want to press charges against these girls, sir? Trespass, breaking-and-entering, attempted burglary—"

"No, no, of course not," he said. He lifted his tear-stained face. "I just want to know that the other kid is all right."

"No one has come out to tell us anything yet," I said in a small voice.

"She lost a lot of blood," Mr. Peegram said. "So much blood..."

"But it was her leg," I broke in. "You can't die from being shot in the leg. Can you?"

"Whose idea was this prank?" Officer O'Rourke asked me in a cold voice.

Should I tell? After all, the Gold Girls really had believed that the house was empty. And they would all hate me forever if I told.

"Mine," I said in a small voice. "It was

my idea. It was so stupid..."

"You're darned right it was stupid," Officer O'Rourke said. "You and your friend are lucky that Mr. Peegram isn't pressing charges, young lady. These are serious offenses."

"Yes, sir," I managed. I looked at Mr. Peegram. "I'm so sorry," I told him again. "We never should have done it."

"I hope you and your friend learn something from this," Officer Paulson said, putting his little notebook away. "You were lucky. You could both be dead right now. And Mr. Peegram here would have been totally within his legal rights."

I nodded, unable to speak.

"If we need any more information, we'll be in touch," Officer O'Rourke said.

"Thank you for your help," my mother said as the officers left.

After that I sank back into the chair and closed my eyes. My mother didn't berate me. She didn't say anything. We all just sat there, waiting for word on Abbie.

After a while—I don't know how long it was—a woman came running into the emergency room. She had bleached blond hair with black roots, and she wore too-tight jeans and a too-tight sweater.

And she looked just like Abbie, only older. Used up.

"My daughter?" she screamed at the nurse who had been so nice. "Abbie Messinger!"

"The doctors are with her now," the nurse said in a soothing voice.

"What happened?" the woman yelled.

I got up and walked over to her. Then I told her what had happened. She started screaming, really going crazy. And when she realized that Bob Peegram was the man who had shot Abbie, she went after him.

Two orderlies had to pull her off him.

"I think you've had a little too much to drink," one of them said to her as he sat her in a chair.

She slumped down, rocking back and forth, moaning softly.

"Go tell her who you are," my mother instructed me.

I did. She looked at me with bloodshot eyes and didn't say a word.

So we all sat there some more. Finally, after what seemed like forever, a doctor came out. He told us Abbie would be okay. She had lost a lot of blood, but the bullet had passed cleanly through her leg. She would have to stay in the hospital for a few days.

After the doctor walked away, my mother turned to Mrs. Messinger. "Is there anything I can do for you?" she asked.

"No," Mrs. Messinger said. "Thanks." Her face looked so sad and ravaged I could hardly stand to look at her.

We drove home. And still my mother hadn't said anything to me. She put the car keys on the desk in the front hall and turned to me. "Something really terrible happened tonight," she said quietly.

I nodded mutely.

"I think you should get some sleep now," my mother said. "We'll talk about it when you wake up. And then we'll go back over to the hospital."

I nodded again, and slowly, so slowly, I trudged upstairs to my room, pulled off my bloody clothes, washed, and climbed into bed. I fell asleep instantly.

Now it was eight hours later. And I was sitting with my mother, staring at a piece of toast. At raspberry jam. Raspberry jam that looked like blood.

"Tell me what happened last night," my mother said.

So I told her. I felt numb, detached from everything. I told her about the Gold Girls, and the initiation. I told her everything.

She was quiet for a moment. "I'm surprised," she finally said. "I've never known you to be a person who follows the crowd."

"I'm not," I said. "I don't know why I did it."

She folded her hands on the table. "I think we should call and tell your father," she said.

"Why?" I asked.

She looked taken aback. "You're his daughter."

"No." I looked out the window as a bird flew by. "Some girl named Kitty is his daughter." I told her about the phone call I'd made to my father.

"I see," she said in a level voice. "So this was a cry for attention from your father."

I turned to her and I felt rage boiling up inside of me. "I don't need him," I said through clenched teeth. "And I don't need you, either."

"Veronica—"

"It's a good thing I don't need either one of you, isn't it?" I asked. "Aren't I supposed to be all grown-up and self-reliant and independent?"

"Really, Veronica—"

"Well, aren't I?" I asked, my voice growing

shrill. "Isn't that what you both want? I don't even know why you had a child in the first place!"

My mother looked stunned. "How can you say that?"

"Because it's true!" I yelled, and tears began to fall down my cheeks. I began to sob so hard that my stomach hurt.

The next thing I knew my mother's arms were around me, and she was rocking me. She hadn't held me like that in a very, very long time.

"I'm sorry," I sobbed, "I'm so sorry, Mom!"

"Shhhh, it's okay, honey," she said. "We'll work it out." She was silent for a long time, just holding me. It felt so good.

Finally I sat back down. She handed me some Kleenex and I blew my nose a lot.

"Veronica, I know that I'm not...a fun person," my mother said stiffly. She stared down at her hands.

I didn't say a word.

"I've always been serious," she continued. "But being serious doesn't mean that I don't love you." Finally she looked at me.

"You never spend any time with me," I said in a small voice.

She took a Kleenex from the box and unconsciously began shredding it in her hands. "I have so many responsibilities at the hospital. It isn't that I don't want to be with you. But now that your father and I have separated..."

"But you did the same thing back in New York," I accused. "Dad did things with me. You never did."

"That's not true!" she said. "Remember that time we all went ice skating together at Rockefeller Center?"

"Mom, I was eight years old," I said. "It was five years ago."

"Was it?" she said faintly. She looked down at the shredded Kleenex and forced herself to put it down on the table. "I will try to spend more time with you."

"Not unless you want to," I said, sounding as stiff as she did.

"I do," she insisted, "but..." She sighed. "Maybe I shouldn't have been a mother. Maybe you're right. Not because I don't love you, because I do..."

I nodded, gulping hard.

"But I don't know if I can ever be the kind of mother you want me to be." Tears came to her eyes. "I'm sorry, Veronica."

I felt so sad. I knew my mother loved me. But it was so hard to hear her tell me I was never going to get the kind of mother I wanted, that it was something she just couldn't do.

And I was just going to have to live with it.

"Abbie?" I whispered, standing next to her bed.

She lay on her back, her eyes closed. Her face was so white it looked like she didn't have any blood.

After the breakfast that I hadn't eaten, my mother had driven me to the hospital. We stopped at a florist on the way. When we got to the hospital, my mother waited in the waiting area while I went into Abbie's room.

Slowly she opened her eyes. "Veronica," she said in a faint voice.

"How are you?" I asked her.

"Okay," she croaked. "I'm tired."

"Does your leg hurt?"

"No," she said. "They gave me some kind of pill thing so it wouldn't."

I pointed awkwardly to the flowers I had brought, which I had put on the windowsill. "I brought those."

"Thanks," she said. "Mr. Peegram was just here."

"He was?"

"He brought me that stuffed bunny." She cocked her head toward a huge blue rabbit that sat next to my flowers on the window-sill.

"Nice," I said lamely. I took a deep breath. "Abbie, I'm so sorry you got hurt—"

"It wasn't your fault," she protested.

"I just feel so terrible—"

"Don't. Really." She shifted her weight in the bed and winced a little. "I have some good news."

"What?"

"Lexi was here this morning, too. Isn't it great that she came to visit me?"

"Sure," I said.

"She was really, really impressed by what we did." Abbie's eyes narrowed with anxiety. "You didn't tell the police about the Gold Girls, did you?"

"No, I didn't."

"Good," Abbie said with relief. "I told Lexi I was sure you wouldn't tell. She says both of us proved we're loyal, that we're willing to do anything for the Gold Girls. I think we're both going to get in! Isn't that great?"

I was so shocked I could hardly answer her. Being in the Gold Girls meant every-thing to her.

It meant more to her than getting shot.

"I hope they take you, Abbie," I said, "if that's what you want."

"They'll take you, too," she said. "I mean, he shot at both of us. You risked your life for the Gold Girls just as much as I did."

It was such crazy thinking! We hadn't meant to risk our lives for Lexi's stupid club. At least I hadn't. Why would I want to be part of a club where the people would want to see me get hurt to prove I was loyal? Cindy and Tina would never in a million years do something like that!

Cindy and Tina. Oh, God. How was I ever going to tell them what I'd done?

After a little while Abbie's mother came in, and I left. Her mother had on those too-tight jeans again, and a sweatshirt with puffy kittens all over it that read "I am the cat's meow."

As I walked out the door, I could hear Abbie's mother yelling at her, cussing her out at the top of her lungs.

My mother would never, ever do anything like that.

Slowly I walked down the hall, back to where my mother was waiting for me. I felt lower than I'd ever felt in my entire life. Everything was so awful. And even though my mother was right out there in the waiting room, once again I felt all alone.

I turned the corner, walking slowly, staring down at my hiking boots, when I heard that sound again.

Thump. Thump. Thump.

It was back again. In the middle of a crowded hospital.

It was the sound of my own heart beating.

Your mother is never going to be the kind of mother you want her to be, it said.

Your father has moved on to another family, it said.

The pain was so awful, I didn't think I could stand it.

Thump. Thump. Thump.

I walked into the waiting room, still staring at my shoes, which were growing blurry through my tears.

"Veronica?"

"Veronica?"

Two different voices.

I looked up.

And there stood the most beautiful sight I had ever seen.

Cindy and Tina, standing right next to my mother.

They held out their arms.

CHAPTER 11

When I could bear to let go of them, I asked them how they had gotten there.

"Your mom called Cindy," Tina explained. "Cindy called me. She told us what happened. She said you needed us."

I looked over at my mother. "Thank you," I said.

She smiled at me. And her eyes were full of love.

Cindy, Tina, and I went to the other side of the room and sat down together.

"Did she tell you everything?" I asked them.

"I think so," Cindy said. "About the Gold

Girls and breaking into the house and everything."

"And someone named Abbie getting shot," Tina added in hushed tones.

"It was so horrible," I said with a shudder. "I just don't know how I could have done anything so stupid. It doesn't even feel like it was me."

"Why didn't you tell us what was going on?" Cindy asked me.

"I tried!" I said. "You had the flu, and you were grounded because you got a bad grade on a test or something..."

"You know my grandmother," Tina said with a sigh. "Anything less than an A is a federal offense. And in my garage, you have to get a ninety-five to get an A."

"And both of you were so busy with your families," I went on. "And I—I don't have a family to be busy with."

"But I still don't get it," Cindy said. She gave me a curious look. "Do you really want to be in with the Gold Girls?"

"No," I said. "I thought I did."

"But why?" Cindy asked. "Those girls are so obnoxious!"

"It's hard to explain," I said slowly. "It—it just seemed like they were really there for each other—"

"I am so sure!" Cindy snorted. "They are only the biggest snobs in the universe! And they're so superficial! I don't think they really care about each other at all!"

"Well, I certainly don't think they really care about me," I said. "Or Abbie."

"*We* care about you," Tina said.

"She already knows that," Cindy said.

"Maybe not," Tina said. "Maybe we need to prove it or something. You know, when I was little, back in San Francisco, I had this best friend. And we vowed we were going to be best friends forever. So we pricked our fingers and rubbed the blood together, and we became blood sisters."

"That's disgusting, Tina Wu!" Cindy cried. "You can get diseases that way!"

"I was five years old," Tina explained with dignity. "I think it was sweet."

Cindy gave me a look. "Please tell me we don't have to, like, cut our flesh open to prove that we love you. I mean, I know we hang out at a hospital, but I can't stand the sight of blood!"

I managed to smile. "You two are crazy, you know that."

"Oh, sure," Tina agreed. "Craziness is one of our better qualities."

"How did you get to the hospital,

137

anyway?" I asked them.

"You're never going to believe this," Tina said. "My grandmother drove us."

"No!" I exclaimed.

"Yes," Tina said. "Cindy's brother had their car. And my mom and dad were at church. I told my grandmother that you were in trouble and you needed me, and she picked up the car keys and drove me to Cindy's house, and then she drove us here."

"You're right, I don't believe it," I said with a little laugh.

"What can I say?" Tina said with a shrug. "My grandmother understands about family."

I felt a lump in my throat. "But I'm not your family."

"Veronica, you idiot," Cindy said. "Of course you are!"

"This is how I see it," Tina said. "When you really, really love a friend, then they're like...like the family that you choose."

Tears came to my eyes again. I didn't feel like I deserved two such incredibly wonderful friends. After all, I had done so many stupid things, and I had made so many mistakes.

But then I realized something. When you love someone, they don't have to be perfect. Sometimes they can't even be who you want them to be. And you keep on loving them, just the same.

I looked across the room at my mother, and our eyes met with love and understanding.

Then I looked back at the two best friends anybody ever had, and I smiled through my tears.

"Don't go getting mushy on us, Veronica," Cindy warned gruffly.

"She can get as mushy as she wants to," Tina said. "I happen to love happy endings."

Then they both put their arms around me. And I knew that no matter what happened with my mother or my father, or all the kids at school who would be so shocked to find out what I had done, I could face it.

Because I wasn't alone.

Dear Cherie,
I loved HOPE HOSPITAL #2 so much, I read it in about two hours. The cheerleaders at my school are really snobby, too. They make fun of people if they are not cool or cute. I'm always afraid that they will decide to make fun of me. What do you think of people who do this?

Lisa Beckwith
Syracuse, New York

Dear Lisa,
Some of the cheerleaders (not all, of course) in my school were like that, too. Wow, did I ever hate it, and I was always afraid they would make fun of me, so I know exactly how you feel. People who make fun of people are insecure and pathetic. It is NEVER cool to do this. I guess they need to make other people feel small in order to make themselves feel bigger. You and your friends should be glad you aren't like them!

Thanks for writing!

Cherie

Dear Cherie,
We are eleven-year-old best friends who love your books. After we read HOPE HOSPITAL #1 we decided to volunteer at our local hospital. So we called up and the hospital said it was okay. We dressed up as clowns and went to the children's ward and made balloon animals for them. It was so much fun. Now we go there once a month. So we just wanted to thank you for giving us this idea!

Carolyn Langelli and Amber White
Sante Fe, New Mexico

Dear Carolyn and Amber,
Wow, that is so cool! I've gotten a number of letters from kids who say they want to volunteer at their local hospital. Here's what you should do: call up and ask to speak to whomever is in charge of volunteers. Tell her about yourself, and that you'd like to volunteer. If you know what you'd like to do at the hospital, tell her and ask if it is possible. Maybe some of you best friends out there can do what Carolyn and Amber are doing! Write and let us know!

Cherie

Dear Reader,

Hi! Time to catch up on all the latest, so here goes....Jeff (for those of you who don't know, that's my very-cute husband) and I just returned from seven weeks in France. For six weeks we were at a writers' retreat, where I wrote a new teen novel and worked on a play. We also spent time in Paris. How many of you guys have been there? It is the most incredible city. If you don't get to go with the parentals, vow to save up and go yourself when you're older. It's worth it!

I've been getting tons of mail about HOPE HOSPITAL, and I'm thrilled that you guys love reading these books as much as I love writing them. Some adults tell me that young people shouldn't read about illness or death, as if that's somehow going to protect you from the experience. But of course we know that isn't true at all. You guys have huge hearts, and you care deeply, and you are to be commended for it. Scary stuff is a part of life, right? And we're here for each other, to help each other through....

As always, I answer each and every letter you send to me. So write to me about HOPE HOSPITAL, or about your life, or your problems, or whatever, and you will hear from me! If you'd like your letter to be considered for publication, *just let me know. If I pick your letter, I'll send you an autographed book as a thank-you.*

You guys are the most wonderful. Hang in there, follow your dreams, and remember...there's always HOPE—

Cherie

Wanna write to me? The address is:
    Cherie Bennett
    PO Box 150326
    Nashville, Tennessee 37215

Wanna E-mail me? And maybe join in on my monthly contest and gab-fest with moi, my cool husband, Jeff, and my readers from all over the world? Contact me at America Online:
        authorchik@aol.com.

Wanna join the Cherie Bennett Believer's Fan Club? Just drop me a note and I'll send you the info!

Cherie Bennett is one of the best-selling authors for young adults and middle readers in the world, with more than three million books in print, in many languages. She is also one of America's finest young playwrights, whose award-winning plays about teens, JOHN LENNON & ME and ANNE FRANK & ME, are being produced around the world. She lives in Nashville, Tennessee, with her husband, Jeff Gottesfeld, a film and theater producer and writer, and their two fat cats, Julius and Trinity.